William Clowes and Sons

Woodland and wild

A selection of descriptive poetry

William Clowes and Sons

Woodland and wild
A selection of descriptive poetry

ISBN/EAN: 9783337278229

Printed in Europe, USA, Canada, Australia, Japan

Cover: Foto ©Andreas Hilbeck / pixelio.de

More available books at **www.hansebooks.com**

WOODLAND AND WILD:

A SELECTION OF DESCRIPTIVE POETRY.

FROM VARIOUS AUTHORS.

WITH NUMEROUS ILLUSTRATIONS ON STEEL AND WOOD.

AFTER ROSA BONHEUR, JULIETTE BONHEUR, CHARLES JACQUE, VEYRASSAT,
YAN DARGENT, AND OTHER ARTISTS.

NEW YORK:

D. APPLETON AND CO., 443 & 445, BROADWAY.

1868.

CONTENTS.

vi   *CONTENTS.*

CONTENTS.

CONTENTS.

LIST OF THE LARGER ILLUSTRATIONS.

WOODLAND AND WILD.

WINTER'S DEPARTURE.

SEE where surly Winter passes off,
  Far to the north, and calls his ruffian blasts;
His blasts obey, and quit the howling hill,
The shatter'd forest and the ravaged vale;
While softer gales succeed, at whose kind touch,
Dissolving snows in livid torrents lost,
The mountains lift their green heads to the sky.

    As yet the trembling year is unconfirm'd,
And winter oft at eve resumes the breeze;
Chills the pale morn, and bids his driving sleets
Deform the day delightless; so that scarce
The bittern knows his time, with bill ungulft
To shake the sounding marsh; or from the shore
The plovers when to scatter o'er the heath,
And sing their wild notes to the listening waste.

    At last from Aries rolls the bounteous sun,
And the bright Bull receives him. Then no more
The expansive atmosphere is cramp'd with cold;
But, full of life and vivifying soul,
Lifts the light clouds sublime; and spreads them thin,
Fleecy and white, o'er all-surrounding heaven.

J. Thomson.

FEBRUARY.

THE snow has left the cottage top;
   The thatch-moss grows in brighter green;
And eaves in quick succession drop,
   Where grinning icicles have been;
Pit-patting with a pleasant noise
   In tubs set by the cottage door;
While ducks and geese, with happy joys,
   Plunge in the yard-pond brimming o'er.

The sun peeps through the window-pane;
   Which children mark with laughing eye,
And in the wet street steal again,
   To tell each other Spring is nigh:
Then, as young hope the past recalls,
   In playing groups they often draw,
To build beside the sunny walls
   Their spring-time huts of sticks or straw.

And oft in pleasure's dreams they hie
   Round homesteads by the village side,
Scratching the hedgerow mosses by,
   Where painted pooty shells abide;

Mistaking oft the ivy spray
   For leaves that come with budding Spring,
And wondering, in their search for play,
   Why birds delay to build and sing.

The milkmaid singing leaves her bed,
   As happy as happy thoughts can be,
While magpies chatter o'er her head
   As jocund in the change as she :
Her cows around the closes stray,
   Nor lingering wait the foddering-boy ;
Tossing the mole-hills in their play,
   And staring round with frolic joy.

The shepherd now is often seen
   Near warm banks o'er his hook to bend ;
Or o'er a gate or stile to lean,
   Chattering to a passing friend :
Ploughmen go whistling to their toils,
   And yoke again the rested plough ;
And, mingling o'er the mellow soils,
   Boys shout, and whips are noising now.

The barking dogs by lane and wood,
   Drive sheep a-field from foddering ground ;
And Echo, in her summer mood,
   Briskly mocks the cheering sound.
The flocks, as from a prison broke,
   Shake their wet fleeces in the sun,
While, following fast, a misty smoke
   Reeks from the moist grass as they run.

No more behind his master's heels
   The dog creeps on his winter-pace ;
But cocks his tail, and o'er the fields
   Runs many a wild and random chase ;

Following, in spite of chiding calls,
　　The startled cat with harmless glee,
Scaring her up the weed-green walls,
　　Or mossy mottled apple-tree.

As crows from morning perches fly,
　　He barks and follows them in vain;
E'en larks will catch his nimble eye,
　　And off he starts and barks again,
With breathless haste and blinded guess,
　　Oft following where the hare hath gone;
Forgetting, in his joy's excess,
　　His frolic puppy-days are done!

The hedgehog, from his hollow root,
　　Sees the wood-moss clear of snow,
And hunts the hedge for fallen fruit—
　　Crab, hip, and winter-bitten sloe;
But often check'd by sudden fears,
　　As shepherd-dog his haunt espies,
He rolls up in a ball of spears,
　　And all his barking rage defies.

The gladden'd swine bolt from the sty,
　　And round the yard in freedom run,
Or stretching in their slumbers lie
　　Beside the cottage in the sun.

The young horse whinneys to his mate,
    And, sickening from the thresher's door,
Rubs at the straw-yard's banded gate,
    Longing for freedom on the moor.

The small birds think their wants are o'er,
    To see the snow-hills fret again,
And, from the barn's chaff-litter'd door,
    Betake them to the greening plain.
The woodman's robin startles coy,
    Nor longer to his elbow comes,
To peck, with hunger's eager joy,
    'Mong mossy stulps the litter'd crumbs.

'Neath hedge and walls that screen the wind,
    The gnats for play will flock together;
And e'en poor flies some hope will find
    To venture in the mocking weather;
From out their hiding-holes again,
    With feeble pace, they often creep
Along the sun-warm'd window-pane,
    Like dreaming things that walk in sleep.

The mavis thrush with wild delight,
    Upon the orchard's dripping tree,
Mutters, to see the day so bright,
    Fragments of young hope's poesy:
And oft dame stops her buzzing wheel
    To hear the robin's note once more,
Who tootles while he pecks his meal
    From sweet-briar hips beside the door.

The sunbeams on the hedges lie,
    The south wind murmurs summer-soft;
The maids hang out white cloths to dry
    Around the elder-skirted croft:

A calm of pleasure listens round,
  And almost whispers Winter by;
While fancy dreams of summer's sound,
  And quiet rapture fills the eye.

Thus nature of the spring will dream
  While south winds thaw; but soon again
Frost breathes upon the stiffening stream,
  And numbs it into ice: the plain
Soon wears its mourning garb of white;
  And icicles, that fret at noon,
Will eke their icy tails at night
  Beneath the chilly stars and moon.

Nature soon sickens of her joys,
  And all is sad and dumb again,
Save merry shouts of sliding boys
  About the frozen furrow'd plain.
The foddering-boy forgets his song,
  And silent goes with folded arms;
And croodling shepherds bend along,
  Crouching to the whizzing storms.

J. Clare.

SPRING.

THE soote * season, that bud and bloom forth brings,
With green hath clad the hill, and eke the vale,
The nightingale with feathers new she sings;
The turtle to her make † hath told her tale.
Summer is come, for every spray now springs.
The hart hath hung his old head on the pale;
The buck in brake his winter coat he flings;
The fishes fleet with new repaired scale;
The adder all her slough away she flings;
The swift swallow pursueth the flies small;
The busy bee her honey now she mings; ‡
Winter is worn that was the flower's bale. §
And thus I see among these pleasant things
Each care decays, and yet my sorrow springs.

Henry Howard, Earl of Surrey.

SPRING.

HE cock is crowing,
   The stream is flowing,
   The small birds twitter,
   The lake doth glitter,
The green field sleeps in the sun;
   The oldest and youngest
   Are at work with the strongest;
   The cattle are grazing,
   Their heads never raising;
There are forty feeding like one!

* Sweet.   † Mate.   ‡ Mingles.   § Destruction.

Like an army defeated
The snow hath retreated,
And now doth fare ill
On the top of the bare hill;
The ploughboy is whooping—anon—anon:
There's joy in the mountains
There's life in the fountains;
Small clouds are sailing,
Blue sky prevailing;
The rain is over and gone!

W. Wordsworth.

SPRING.

Now that the winter's gone, the earth hath lost
Her snow-white robes, and now no more the frost
Candies the grass, or casts an icy cream
Upon the silver lake, or crystal stream:
But the warm sun thaws the benumbed earth
And makes it tender, gives a sacred birth
To the dead swallow, wakes in hollow tree

The drowsy cuckoo and the humble bee.
Now do a choir of chirping minstrels bring
In triumph to the world, the youthful spring:
The valleys, hills, and woods, in rich array,
Welcome the coming of the long'd-for May.

T. Carew.

THE STARLINGS.

EARLY in spring time, on raw and windy mornings,
Beneath the freezing house-eaves I heard the starlings sing—
'Ah dreary March month, is this then a time for building wearily?
Sad, sad, to think that the year has but begun.'

Late in the autumn, on still and cloudless evenings,
Among the golden reed-beds I heard the starlings sing—
'Ah that sweet March month, when we and our mates were courting
    merrily:
Sad, sad, to think that the year is all but done.'

C. Kingsley.

SPRING.

FROST-LOCKED all the winter,
Seeds, and roots, and stones of fruits,
What shall make their sap ascend
That they may put forth shoots?
Tips of tender green,
Leaf, or blade, or sheath;
Telling of the hidden life
That breaks forth underneath,
Life nursed in its grave by Death.

Blows the thaw-wind pleasantly,
Drips the soaking rain,
By fits looks down the waking sun:
Young grass springs on the plain;
Young leaves clothe early hedgerow trees;
Seeds, and roots, and stones of fruits,
Swollen with sap put forth their shoots;
Curled-headed ferns sprout in the lane;
Birds sing and pair again.

C

There is no time like Spring,
When life's alive in everything,
Before new nestlings sing,
Before cleft swallows speed their journey back
Along the trackless track—
God guides their wing;
He spreads their table that they nothing lack,—
Before the daisy grows a common flower,
Before the sun has power
To scorch the world up in his noontide hour.

There is no time like Spring—
Like Spring that passes by;
There is no life like Spring-life born to die,—
Piercing the sod,
Clothing the uncouth clod,
Hatched in the nest,
Fledged on the windy bough,
Strong on the wing:
There is no time like Spring that passes by,
Now newly born, and now
Hastening to die.

Christina Rossetti.

SPRING IN AMERICA.

WINTER is past; the heart of Nature warms
Beneath the wrecks of unresisted storms;
Doubtful at first, suspected more than seen,
The southern slopes are fringed with tender green;
On sheltered banks, beneath the dripping eaves,
Spring's earliest nurslings spread their glowing leaves,
Bright with the hues from wider pictures won,
White, azure, golden,—drift, or sky, or sun;—
The snowdrop, bearing on her patient breast
The frozen trophy torn from winter's crest;
The violet, gazing on the arch of blue
Till her own iris wears its deepened hue;
The spendthrift crocus, bursting through the mould
Naked and shivering with his cup of gold.
Swelled with new life, the darkening elm on high
Prints her thick buds against the spotted sky;
On all her boughs the stately chestnut cleaves
The gummy shroud that wraps her embryo leaves;
The house-fly, stealing from his narrow grave,
Drugged with the opiate that November gave,
Beats with faint wing against the sunny pane,
Or crawls, tenacious, o'er its lucid plain;
From shaded chinks of lichen-crusted walls,
In languid curves, the gliding serpent crawls;
The bog's green harper, thawing from his sleep,
Twangs a hoarse note and tries a shortened leap;
On floating rails that face the softening noons
The still shy turtles range their dark platoons,
Or toiling, aimless, o'er the mellowing fields,
Trail through the grass their tesselated shields.

O. Wendell Holmes.

THE WOODLAND.

THEY came to where the brushwood ceased, and day
Peer'd 'twixt the stems; and the ground broke away
In a sloped sward down to a brawling brook,
And up as high as where they stood to look
On the brook's further side was clear; but there
The underwood and trees began again.
This open glen was studded thick with thorns
Then white with blossom; and you saw the horns,
Through the green fern, of the shy fallow-deer,
Which come at noon down to the water here.
You saw the bright-eyed squirrels dart along
Under the thorns on the green sward; and strong
The blackbird whistled from the dingles near,
And the light chipping of the woodpecker
Rang lonelily and sharp; the sky was fair,
And a fresh breath of spring stirred everywhere.
Merlin and Vivian stopp'd on the slope's brow
To gaze on the green sea of leaf and bough
Which glittering lay all round them, lone and mild,
As if to itself the quiet forest smiled.
Upon the brow-top grew a thorn; and here
The grass was dry and moss'd, and you saw clear.
Across the hollow: white anemones
Starr'd the cool turf, and clumps of primroses
Ran out from the dark underwood behind.
No fairer resting-place a man could find.

Matthew Arnold.

THE CUCKOO.

BLITHE new-comer! I have heard,
    I hear thee and rejoice.
O Cuckoo! shall I call thee bird,
    Or but a wandering voice?

While I am lying on the grass
    Thy twofold shout I hear,
From hill to hill it seems to pass,
    At once far off, and near.

Though babbling only to the vale,
    Of sunshine and of flowers,
Thou bringest unto me a tale
    Of visionary hours.

Thrice welcome, darling of the Spring!
    Even yet thou art to me
No bird, but an invisible thing,
    A voice, a mystery;

The same whom in my schoolboy days
    I listened to; that cry
Which made me look a thousand ways
    In bush, and tree, and sky.

To seek thee did I often rove
    Through woods and on the green;
And thou wert still a hope, a love;
    Still longed for, never seen.

And can I listen to thee yet;
    Can lie upon the plain
And listen, till I do beget
    That golden time again.

O blessed bird! the earth we pace
  Again appears to be
An unsubstantial, faery place;
  That is fit home for thee.

                    W. Wordsworth.

THE CUCKOO.

Hail, beauteous stranger of the grove!
  Thou messenger of spring!
Now heaven repairs thy rural seat,
  And woods thy welcome sing.

What time the daisy decks the green,
  Thy certain voice we hear;
Hast thou a star to guide thy path,
  Or mark the rolling year?

Delightful visitant! with thee
  I hail the time of flowers,
And hear the sound of music sweet
  From birds among the bowers.

The school-boy wandering through the wood,
  To pull the primrose gay,
Starts, the new voice of spring to hear,
  And imitates thy lay.

What time the pea puts on the bloom
  Thou fliest thy vocal vale,
An annual guest in other lands,
  Another spring to hail.

Sweet bird! thy bower is ever green,
   Thy sky is ever clear;
Thou hast no sorrow in thy song,
   No winter in thy year!

O could I fly, I'd fly with thee!
   We'd make, with joyful wing,
Our annual visit o'er the globe,
   Companions of the spring.

                                         J. Logan.

THE SONG-BIRD.

WEET bird, that sing'st away the early hours,
Of winters past or coming void of care,
Well pleased with delights which present are,
Fair seasons, budding sprays, sweet-smelling flowers;
To rocks, to springs, to rills, from leafy bowers
Thou thy Creator's goodness dost declare,
And what dear gifts on thee He did not spare;
A stain to human sense in sin that lowers.
What soul can be so sick, which by thy songs,
Attired in sweetness, sweetly is not driven
Quite to forget earth's turmoils, spites and wrongs,
And lift a reverent eye and thought to heaven?
   Sweet, artless songster, thou my mind dost raise
   To airs of spheres, yea, and to angels' lays.

                                      W. Drummond.

BLOSSOMS.

FAIR pledges of a fruitful tree,
  Why do ye fall so fast?
  Your date is not so past,
But you may stay yet here awhile,
  To blush and gently smile,
    And go at last.

What, were ye born to be
  An hour or half's delight,
  And so to bid good-night?
'Twas pity nature brought ye forth,
  Merely to show your worth,
    And lose you quite.

But you are lovely leaves, where we
  May read how soon things have
  Their end, though ne'er so brave;
And after they have shown their pride
  Like you awhile, they glide
    Into the grave.

R. Herrick.

THE DAFFODILS.

WANDERED lonely as a cloud
That floats on high o'er vales and hills,
When all at once I saw a crowd,
A host, of golden daffodils;
Beside the lake, beneath the trees,
Fluttering and dancing in the breeze.

Continuous as the stars that shine
And twinkle on the Milky-way,
They stretched in never-ending line
Along the margin of a bay:
Ten thousand saw I at a glance,
Tossing their heads in sprightly dance.

The waves beside them danced; but they
Out-did the sparkling waves in glee:
A poet could not but be gay,
In such a jocund company:
I gazed—and gazed—but little thought
What wealth the show to me had brought:

For oft, when on my couch I lie
In vacant or in pensive mood,
They flash upon that inward eye
Which is the bliss of solitude;
And then my heart with pleasure fills,
And dances with the daffodils.

W. Wordsworth.

THE DAFFODILS.

Fair Daffodils, we weep to see
    You haste away so soon;
As yet the early rising sun
    Has not attain'd his noon.
        Stay, stay,
    Until the hasting day
        Has run
    But to the even-song;
And, having pray'd together, we
    Will go with you along.

We have short time to stay as you,
    We have as short a spring;
As quick a growth to meet decay,
    As you, or anything.
        We die
    As your hours do, and dry
        Away,
    Like to the summer's rain;
Or as the pearls of morning's dew,
    Ne'er to be found again.

                R. Herrick.

MAY MORNING.

Now the bright morning star, day's harbinger,
Comes dancing from the east, and leads with her
The flowery May, who from her green lap throws
The yellow cowslip, and the pale primrose.
    Hail, bounteous May, that dost inspire
    Mirth and youth, and warm desire;
    Woods and groves are of thy dressing,
    Hill and dale doth boast thy blessing.
Thus we salute thee with our early song,
And welcome thee, and wish thee long.

                J. Milton.

THE NIGHTINGALE.

No cloud, no relique of the sunken day
Distinguishes the West—no long thin slip
Of sullen light, no obscure trembling hues.
Come, we will rest on this old mossy bridge!
You see the glimmer of the stream beneath.
But hear no murmuring: it flows silently,
O'er its soft bed of verdure. All is still,
A balmy night! and though the stars be dim,
Yet let us think upon the vernal showers
That gladden the green earth, and we shall find
A pleasure in the dimness of the stars.
And hark! the nightingale begins its song,
"Most musical, most melancholy" bird!
A melancholy bird! Oh! idle thought!
In Nature there is nothing melancholy.
But some night-wandering man whose heart was pierced
With the remembrance of a grievous wrong,
Or slow distemper, or neglected love,
(And so, poor wretch! filled all things with himself,
And made all gentle sounds tell back the tale
Of his own sorrow) he, and such as he,
First named these notes a melancholy strain.
And many a poet echoes the conceit;
Poet who hath been building up the rhyme
When he had better far have stretched his limbs
Beside a brook in mossy forest-dell,
By sun or moonlight, to the influxes
Of shapes and sounds and shifting elements
Surrendering his whole spirit, of his song
And of his fame forgetful! So his fame
Should share in Nature's immortality,
A venerable thing! and so his song
Should make all Nature lovelier, and itself
Beloved like Nature! But 'twill not be so;
And youths and maidens most poetical,

Who lose the deepening twilights of the spring
In ball-rooms and hot theatres, they still,
Full of meek sympathy, must heave their sighs
O'er Philomela's pity-pleading strains.

      My friend, and thou, our sister! we have learnt
A different lore: we may not thus profane
Nature's sweet voices, always full of love
And joyance! 'Tis the merry nightingale
That crowds, and hurries, and precipitates
With fast thick warble his delicious notes,
As he were fearful that an April night
Would be too short for him to utter forth
His love-chant, and disburthen his full soul
Of all its music!

      And I know a grove
Of large extent, hard by a castle huge,
Which the great lord inhabits not; and so
This grove is wild with tangling underwood,
And the trim walks are broken up, and grass,
Thin grass, and king-cups grow within the paths.
But never elsewhere in one place I knew
So many nightingales; and far and near,
In wood and thicket, over the wide grove,
They answer and provoke each other's song,
With skirmish and capricious passagings,
And murmurs musical and swift jug-jug,
And one low piping sound more sweet than all—
Stirring the air with such a harmony,
That should you close your eyes, you might almost
Forget it was not day! On moon-lit bushes,
Whose dewy leaflets are but half disclosed,
You may perchance behold them on the twigs,
Their bright, bright eyes, their eyes both bright and full,
Glistening, while many a glow-worm in the shade
Lights up her love-torch.

      A most gentle maid,
Who dwelleth in her hospitable home

Hard by the castle, and at latest eve
(Even like a lady vowed and dedicate
To something more than Nature in the grove)
Glides through the pathways; she knows all their notes,
That gentle maid! and oft a moment's space,
What time the moon was lost behind a cloud,
Hath heard a pause of silence; till the moon
Emerging, hath awakened earth and sky
With one sensation, and these wakeful birds
Have all burst forth in choral minstrelsy,
As if some sudden gale had swept at once
A hundred airy harps! And she hath watched
Many a nightingale perched giddily
On blossomy twig still swinging from the breeze,
And to that motion tune his wanton song
Like tipsy joy that reels with tossing head.

Farewell, O warbler! till to-morrow eve,
And you, my friends, farewell, a short farewell!
We have been loitering long and pleasantly,
And now for our dear homes.—That strain again!
Full fain it would delay me! My dear babe,
Who, capable of no articulate sound,
Mars all things with his imitative lisp,
How he would place his hand beside his ear,
His little hand, the small forefinger up,
And bid us listen! And I deem it wise
To make him Nature's play-mate. He knows well
The evening star; and once, when he awoke
In most distressful mood (some inward pain
Had made up that strange thing, an infant's dream),
I hurried with him to our orchard-plot,
And he beheld the moon, and, hushed at once,
Suspends his sobs, and laughs most silently,
While his fair eyes, that swam with undropped tears,
Did glitter in the yellow moonbeam! Well!
It is a father's tale. But if that Heaven

Should give me life, his childhood shall grow up
Familiar with these songs, that with the night
He may associate joy. Once more, farewell,
Sweet nightingale! Once more, my friends, farewell!

S. T. Coleridge.

FLOWERS AND BIRDS.

ROSES, their sharp spines being gone,
    Not royal in their smells alone,
      But in their hue;
Maiden pinks, of odour faint,
Daisies smell-less, yet most quaint,
      And sweet thyme true;

Primrose, first-born child of Ver,
Merry spring-time's harbinger,
      With her bells dim:
Oxlips in their cradles growing,
Marigolds on death-beds blowing,
      Lark-heels trim;

All, dear Nature's children sweet,
Lie 'fore bride and bridegroom's feet,
    Blessing their sense!
Not an angel of the air,
Bird melodious, or bird fair,
    Be absent hence!

The crow, the slanderous cuckoo, nor
The boding raven, nor chough hoar,
    Nor chattering pie,
May on our bride-house perch or sing,
Or with them any discord bring,
    But from it fly!

J. Fletcher.

THE SKY-LARK.

H! Sky-lark, for thy wing!
  Thou bird of joy and light,
That I might soar and sing
  At heaven's empyreal height!
With the heathery hills beneath me,
  Whence the streams in glory spring,
And the pearly clouds to wreath me,
  Oh Sky-lark! on thy wing!

Free, free from earth-born fear,
  I would range the blessed skies,
Through the blue divinely clear,
  Where the low mists cannot rise!
And a thousand joyous measures
  From my chainless heart should spring,
Like the bright rain's vernal treasures,
  As I wandered on thy wing.

But oh! the silver chords,
  That around the heart are spun,
From gentle tones and words,
  And kind eyes that make our sun!
To some low sweet nest returning,
  How soon my love would bring,
There, *there* the dews of morning,
  Oh, Sky-lark! on thy wing!

Felicia Hemans.

TO A SKYLARK.

HAIL to thee, blithe spirit!
  Bird thou never wert,
That from heaven, or near it,
  Pourest thy full heart
In profuse strains of unpremeditated art.

  Higher still and higher,
    From the earth thou springest
  Like a cloud of fire;
    The blue deep thou wingest,
And singing still dost soar, and soaring ever singest.

  In the golden lightning
    Of the sunken sun,
  O'er which clouds are brightening,
    Thou dost float and run;
Like an unbodied joy whose race is just begun.

  The pale purple even
    Melts around thy flight;
  Like a star of heaven,
    In the broad daylight
Thou art unseen, but yet I hear thy shrill delight.

  Keen as are the arrows
    Of that silver sphere,
  Whose intense lamp narrows
    In the white dawn clear,
Until we hardly see, we feel that it is there.

  All the earth and air
    With thy voice is loud,
  As, when night is bare,
    From one lonely cloud
The moon rains out her beams, and heaven is overflowed.

What thou art we know not;
　　What is most like thee?
From rainbow clouds there flow not
　　Drops so bright to see,
As from thy presence showers a rain of melody.

Like a poet hidden
　　In the light of thought,
Singing hymns unbidden
　　Till the world is wrought
To sympathy with hopes and fears it heeded not:

Like a high-born maiden
　　In a palace tower,
Soothing her love-laden
　　Soul in secret hour
With music sweet as love, which overflows her bower:

Like a glowworm golden
　　In a dell of dew,
Scattering unbeholden
　　Its aëreal hue
Among the flowers and grass, which screen it from the view:

Like a rose embowered
　　In its own green leaves,
By warm winds deflowered,
　　Till the scent it gives
Makes faint with too much sweet these heavy-winged thieves.

Sound of vernal showers
　　On the twinkling grass,
Rain-awakened flowers,
　　All that ever was
Joyous and clear, and fresh, thy music doth surpass.

Teach us, sprite or bird,
　　What sweet thoughts are thine:
I have never heard
　　Praise of love or wine
That panted forth a flood of rapture so divine.

E

Chorus hymeneal,
  Or triumphal chaunt,
Matched with thine would be all
  But an empty vaunt—
A thing wherein we feel there is some hidden want.

  What objects are the fountains
    Of thy happy strain?
  What fields, or waves, or mountains?
    What shapes of sky or plain?
What love of thine own kind? what ignorance of pain?

  With thy clear keen joyance
    Languor cannot be:
  Shadow of annoyance
    Never came near thee:
Thou lovest, but ne'er knew love's sad satiety.

  Waking or asleep,
    Thou of death must deem
  Things more true and deep
    Than we mortals dream,
Or how could thy notes flow in such a crystal stream?

  We look before and after,
    And pine for what is not:
  Our sincerest laughter
    With some pain is fraught;
Our sweetest songs are those that tell of saddest thought.

  . Yet if we could scorn
    Hate, and pride, and fear;
  If we were things born
    Not to shed a tear,
I know not how thy joy we ever should come near.

  Better than all measures
    Of delightful sound,
  Better than all treasures
    That in books are found,
Thy skill to poet were, thou scorner of the ground!

Teach me half the gladness
  That thy brain must know,
Such harmonious madness
  From my lips would flow,
The world should listen then, as I am listening now.
P. B. Shelley.

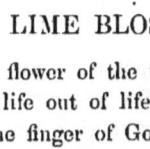

LIME BLOSSOMS.

THE flower of the tree is the flower for me,
That life out of life, high-hanging and free,
By the finger of God and the south wind's fan
Drawn from the broad bough, as Eve from Man!
From the rank red earth it never up-grew;—
It was woo'd from the bark in the breezy blue.

Hail, blossoms green 'mid the limes unseen,
  That charm the bees to your honey'd screen,
As like to the green trees that gave you birth
As noble manners to inward worth!
We see you not; but, we scarce know why,
We are glad when the air ye have breathed goes by.

O flowers of the lime! 'twas a merry time
When under you first we read old rhyme,
And heard the wind roam over pale and park,
(*We* 'not I) 'mid the lime-grove dark!
Summer is heavy and sad. Ye bring
With your tardy blossoms a second spring.
Aubrey de Vere.

SUMMER.

INTER is cold-hearted,
  Spring is yea and nay,
Autumn is a weathercock
  Blown every way:
Summer days for me
  When every leaf is on its tree;

When Robin's not a beggar,
  And Jenny Wren's a bride,
And larks hang singing, singing, singing,
  Over the wheat-fields wide,
  And anchored lilies ride,
And the pendulum spider
  Swings from side to side,

And blue-black beetles transact business,
  And gnats fly in a host,
And furry caterpillars hasten
  That no time be lost,
And moths grow fat and thrive,
And ladybirds arrive.

Before green apples blush,
  Before green nuts embrown,
Why, one day in the country
  Is worth a month in town;
  Is worth a day and a year
Of the dusty, musty, lag-last fashion
  That days drone elsewhere.

Christina Rossetti.

A SUMMER DAY.

I STOOD tiptoe upon a little hill,
The air was cooling, and so very still,
That the sweet buds which with a modest pride
Pull droopingly, in slanting curve aside,
Their scanty-leaved, and finely-tapering stems,
Had not yet lost their starry diadems
Caught from the early sobbing of the morn.
The clouds were pure and white as flocks new-shorn,
And fresh from the clear brook; sweetly they slept
On the blue fields of heaven, and then there crept
A little noiseless noise among the leaves,
Born of the very sigh that silence heaves;
For not the faintest motion could be seen
Of all the shades that slanted o'er the green.
There was wide wandering for the greediest eye,
To peer about upon variety;
Far round the horizon's crystal air to skim,
And trace the dwindled edgings of its brim;
To picture out the quaint and curious bending
Of a fresh woodland alley never-ending:
Or by the bowery clefts, and leafy shelves,
Guess where the jaunty streams refresh themselves.
I gazed awhile, and felt as light and free
As though the fanning wings of Mercury
Had play'd upon my heels: I was light-hearted,
And many pleasures to my vision started;
So I straightway began to pluck a posy
Of luxuries bright, milky, soft and rosy.
A bush of May-flowers with the bees about them;
Ah, sure no tasteful nook could be without them!
And let a lush laburnum oversweep them,
And let long grass grow round the roots, to keep them
Moist, cool and green; and shade the violets,
That they may bind the moss in leafy nets.

A filbert-hedge with wildbriar overtwined,
And clumps of woodbine taking the soft wind
Upon their summer thrones; there too should be
The frequent chequer of a youngling tree,
That with a score of light green brethren shoots
From the quaint mossiness of aged roots:
Round which is heard a spring-head of clear waters,
Babbling so wildly of its lovely daughters,
The spreading blue-bells; it may haply mourn
That such fair clusters should be rudely torn
From their fresh beds, and scatter'd thoughtlessly
By infant hands, left on the path to die.

    *   *   *   *   *

Here are sweet peas, on tiptoe for a flight:
With wings of gentle flush o'er delicate white,
And taper fingers catching at all things,
To bind them all about with tiny rings.
Linger awhile upon some bending planks

That lean against a streamlet's rushy banks,
And watch intently Nature's gentle doings:
They will be found softer than ring-doves' cooings.
How silent comes the water round that bend!
Not the minutest whisper does it send

To the o'erhanging sallows : blades of grass
Slowly across the chequer'd shadows pass.
Why you might read two sonnets, ere they reach
To where the hurrying freshnesses aye preach
A natural sermon o'er their pebbly beds ;
Where swarms of minnows show their little heads,
Staying their wavy bodies 'gainst the streams,
To taste the luxury of sunny beams
Temper'd with coolness.   How they ever wrestle
With their own sweet delight, and ever nestle
Their silver bellies on the pebbly sand !
If you but scantily hold out the hand,
That very instant not one will remain ;
But turn your eye, and they are there again.
The ripples seem right glad to reach those cresses,
And cool themselves among the emerald tresses ;
The while they cool themselves, they freshness give,
And moisture, that the bowery green may live :
So keeping up an interchange of favours,
Like good men in the truth of their behaviours.
Sometimes goldfinches one by one will drop
From low-hung branches : little space they stop ;
But sip, and twitter, and their feathers sleek ;
Then off at once, as in a wanton freak :
Or perhaps, to show their black and golden wings,
Pausing upon their yellow flutterings.
Were I in such a place, I sure should pray
That nought less sweet might call my thoughts away
Than the soft rustle of a maiden's gown
Fanning away the dandelion's down ;
Than the light music of her nimble toes
Patting against the sorrel as she goes.
How she would start, and blush, thus to be caught
Playing in all her innocence of thought !
O let me lead her gently o'er the brook,
Watch her half-smiling lips and downward look ;
O let me for one moment touch her wrist,
Let me one moment to her breathing list ;

And as she leaves me, may she often turn
Her fair eyes looking through her locks auburne.
What next? A tuft of evening primroses,
O'er which the mind may hover till it dozes;
O'er which it well might take a pleasant sleep,
But that 'tis ever startled by the leap
Of buds into ripe flowers; or by the flitting
Of divers moths, that aye their rest are quitting;
Or by the moon lifting her silver rim
Above a cloud, and with a gradual swim
Coming into the blue with all her light.

J. Keats.

SUNRISE ON THE HILLS.

STOOD upon the hills, when heaven's wide arch
Was glorious with the sun's returning march,
And woods were brightened, and soft gales
Went forth to kiss the sun-clad vales.
The clouds were far beneath me ;—bathed in light,
They gathered mid-way round the wooded height,
And, in their fading glory, shone
Like hosts in battle overthrown,
As many a pinnacle, with shifting glance,
Through the gray mist thrust up its shattered lance,
And rocking on the cliff was left
The dark pine blasted, bare, and cleft,
The veil of cloud was lifted, and below
Glowed the rich valley, and the river's flow
Was darkened by the forest's shade,
Or glistened in the wide cascade ;
Where, upward in the mellow blush of day,
The noisy bittern wheeled his spiral way.

I heard the distant waters dash,
I saw the current whirl and flash,
And richly, by the blue lake's silver beach,
The woods were bending with a silent reach.
Then o'er the vale, with gentle swell,
The music of the village bell
Came sweetly to the echo-giving hills:
And the wild horn, whose voice the woodland fills,
Was ringing to the merry shout,
That faint and far the glen sent out,
Where, answering to the sudden shot, thin smoke,
Through thick-leaved branches, from the dingle broke.

If thou art worn and hard beset
With sorrows that thou wouldst forget,
If thou wouldst read a lesson that will keep
Thy heart from fainting and thy soul from sleep,
Go to the woods and hills! No tears
Dim the sweet look that nature wears.

H. W. Longfellow.

A SUMMER MORN.

To yonder hill, whose sides, deform'd and steep
Just yield a scanty sustenance to the sheep,
With thee, my friend, I oftentimes have sped,
To see the sun rise from his healthy bed;
To watch the aspect of the summer morn,
Smiling upon the golden fields of corn,
And taste delighted of superior joys,
Beheld through Sympathy's enchanted eyes:
With silent admiration oft we view'd
The myriad hues o'er heaven's blue concave strew'd;

F

The fleecy clouds, of every tint and shade,
Round which the silvery sunbeam glancing play'd,
And the round orb itself, in azure throne,
Just peeping o'er the blue hill's ridgy zone;
We mark'd delighted, how with aspect gay,
Reviving Nature hail'd returning day;
Mark'd how the flowerets rear'd their drooping heads,
And the wild lambkins bounded o'er the meads,
While from each tree, in tones of sweet delight,
The birds sung pæans to the source of light:
Oft have we watch'd the speckled lark arise,
Leave his grass bed, and soar to kindred skies,
And rise, and rise, till the pained sight no more
Could trace him in his high aërial tour;
Though on the ear, at intervals, his song
Came wafted slow the wavy breeze along;
And we have thought how happy were our lot,
Bless'd with some sweet, some solitary cot,
Where, from the peep of day, till russet eve
Began in every dell her forms to weave,
We might pursue our sports from day to day,
And in each other's arms wear life away.

H. Kirke White.

SUMMER MOODS.

I LOVE at eventide to walk alone,
  Down narrow lanes o'erhung with dewy thorn,
Where from the long grass underneath, the snail
  Jet black creeps out and sprouts his timid horn.
I love to muse o'er meadows newly mown,
  Where withering grass perfumes the sultry air;

Where bees search round with sad and weary drone,
　In vain for flowers that bloomed but newly there;
While in the juicy corn, the hidden quail
　Cries "Wet my foot!" and, hid as thoughts unborn,
The fairy-like and seldom seen land-rail
　Utters "Craik, craik!" like voices underground:
Right glad to meet the evening's dewy veil,
　And see the light fade into glooms around.

J. Clare.

THE EVENING STAR.

STAR that bringest home the bee,
And sett'st the weary labourer free!
If any star shed peace, 'tis thou,
　That send'st it from above,
Appearing when heaven's breath and brow
　Are sweet as hers we love.

Come to the luxuriant skies,
Whilst the landscape's odours rise,
Whilst far-off lowing herds are heard,
　And songs, when toil is done,
From cottages whose smoke unstirred
　Curls yellow in the sun.

Star of love's soft interviews,
Parted lovers on thee muse;
Their remembrancer in heaven
  Of thrilling vows thou art,
Too delicious to be riven
  By absence from the heart.

T. Campbell.

EVENING.

If aught of oaten stop, or pastoral song,
May hope, O pensive Eve! to soothe thine ear,
  Like thy own brawling springs,
  Thy springs and dying gales.

O nymph reserved! while now the bright-hair'd sun
Sits in yon western tent, whose cloudy skirts,
  With brede ethereal wove,
  O'erhang his wavy bed:

Now air is hush'd, save where the weak-eyed bat,
With short shrill shriek flits by on leathern wing;
  Or where the beetle winds
  His small but sullen horn.

As oft he rises 'midst the twilight path,
Against the pilgrim borne in heedless hum:
  Now teach me, maid composed,
  To breathe some soften'd strain,

Whose numbers, stealing thro' thy darkening vale,
May not unseemly with its stillness suit,
  As musing slow, I hail,
  Thy genial, loved return!

For when thy folding-star arising shows
His paly circlet at his warning lamp,
   The fragrant hours, and elves
   Who slept in buds the day,

And many a nymph, who wreathes her brows with sedge,
And sheds the freshening dews, and, lovelier still,
   The pensive Pleasures sweet,
   Prepare thy shadowy car.

Then let me rove some wild and heathy scene;
Or find some ruin, 'midst its dreary dells,
   Whose walls more awful nod
   By thy religious gleams.

Or, if chill blustering winds, or driving rain,
Prevent my willing feet, be mine the hut,
   That, from the mountain's side,
   Views wilds, and swelling floods,

And hamlets brown, and dim-discover'd spires,
And hears their simple bell, and marks o'er all
   Thy dewy fingers draw
   The gradual dusky veil.

While Spring shall pour his showers, as oft he wont,
And bathe thy breathing tresses, meekest Eve!
　　While summer loves to sport
　　Beneath thy lingering light;

While sallow Autumn fills thy lap with leaves,
Or Winter, yelling through the troublous air,
　　Affrights thy shrinking train,
　　And rudely rends thy robes;

So long, regardful of thy quiet rule,
Shall Fancy, Friendship, Science, smiling Peace,
　　Thy gentlest influence own,
　　And love thy favourite name!

　　　　　　　　　　　　　　　　　W. Collins.

MILKEN TIME.*

'Twer when the busy birds did vlee,
Wi' sheenèn wings, vrom tree to tree,
To build upon the mossy lim',
Their hollow nestes' rounded rim;
The while the zun, a-zinkèn low,
Did roll along his evenèn bow,
I come along where wide-horn'd cows,
'Ithin a nook, a-screen'd by boughs,
Did stan' an' flip the white-hoop'd païls,
Wi' heäiry tufts o' swingèn taïls;
An' there wer Jenny Coom a-gone
Along the path a vew steps on,
A-beärèn on her head, up-straïght,
Her païl, wi' slowly-ridèn waïght,

---

* This poem and that on "Hay Miaken" are taken, by permission, from *Poems in the Dorset-shire dialect*. By the Rev. W. Barnes, 3 vols. J. R. Smith, Soho Square.

An' hoops a-sheenèn, lily-white,
Ageän the evenèn's slantèn light;
An' zo I took her païl, an' left
Her neck a-freed vrom all its heft;
An' she a-lookèn up an' down,
Wi' sheäply head an' glossy crown,
Then took my zide, an' kept my peäce
A-talkèn on wi' smilèn feäce,
An' zettèn things in sich a light,
I'd faïn ha' heär'd her talk all night;
An' when I brought her milk avore
The geäte, she took it in to door,
An' if her païl had but allow'd
Her head to vall, she would ha' bow'd,
An' still, as 'twer, I had the zight
Ov her sweet smile droughout the night.

        W. Barnes.

EVENING.

HEPHERDS all, and maidens fair,
Fold your flocks up, for the air
'Gins to thicken, and the sun
Already his great course hath run.
See the dewdrops how they kiss
Every little flower that is;
Hanging on their velvet heads,
Like a rope of crystal beads.
See the heavy clouds low falling,
And bright Hesperus down calling
The dead Night from under ground;
At whose rising mists unsound,
Damps and vapours fly apace,
Hovering o'er the wanton face
Of these pastures, where they come,
Striking dead both bud and bloom.

Therefore, from such danger, lock
Every one his loved flock;
And let your dogs lie loose without,
Lest the wolf come as a scout
From the mountain, and ere day
Bear a lamb or kid away;
Or the crafty thievish fox
Break upon your simple flocks.
To secure yourselves from these,
Be not too secure in ease;
Let one eye his watches keep,
While the other eye doth sleep;
So you shall good shepherds prove,
And for ever hold the love
Of our great God. Sweetest slumbers,
And soft silence, fall in numbers
On your eyelids! So, farewell!
Thus I end my evening's knell.

J. Fletcher.

SUNSET.

YET the rich blessing which this hour bestows
Let us not mar with mournful thoughts like these:
See yonder where the sun of evening glows,
How gleam the green-girt cottages!
He stoops, he sinks—and overlived is day;
But he hastes on, to kindle life anew.
Ah! that no wing lifts me from earth away
Him to pursue, and evermore pursue:
Then should I in eternal evening light
The hushed world at my feet behold,
See every vale in calm, and flaming every height,
And silver brooks see lost in floods of gold.

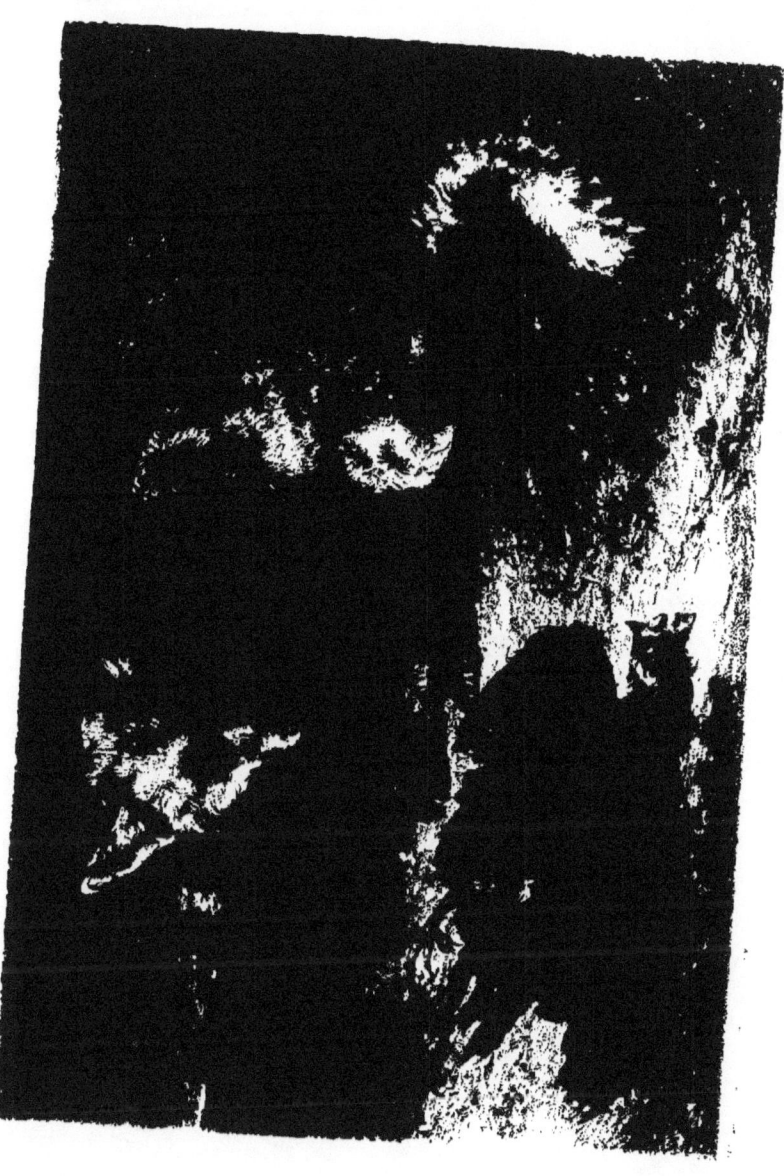

Then would not the wild mountain hinder more
My course divine with all its rugged heads:
Its heated bays even now the ocean spreads
My wondering eyes before.
Yet the god seems at last away to sink;
But the new impulse stirs with might:
I hasten his eternal beams to drink,
The day before me, and behind the night,
The heaven above me spread, and under me the sea:
Fair dream! which while I dream on, he is gone.
Ah! that an actual wing may not so soon
Unto our spirit's wing united be,
And yet it is to each inbred.
That still his spirit forward, upward springs,
When hidden in blue spaces overhead
The lark his shattering carol sings;
When over pine-clad mountains soars
The eagle, spread upon the air,
When over seas and over moors
The crane doth to its home repair.

Archbishop Trench.
From the German of Goethe.

TWILIGHT CALM.

O, PLEASANT eventide!
Clouds on the western side
Grow grey and greyer hiding the warm sun:
The bees and birds, their happy labours done,
Seek their close nests and bide.

Screened in the leafy wood
The stockdoves sit and brood:
The very squirrel leaps from bough to bough
But lazily; pauses; and settles now
Where once he stored his food.

G

One by one the flowers close,
  Lily and dewy rose
Shutting their tender petals from the moon :
The grasshoppers are still ; but not so soon
  Are still the noisy crows.

  The dormouse squats and eats
  Choice little dainty bits
Beneath the spreading roots of a broad lime ;
Nibbling his fill, he stops from time to time
  And listens where he sits.

  From far the lowings come
  Of cattle driven home :
From farther still the wind brings fitfully
The vast continual murmur of the sea,
  Now loud, now almost dumb.

  The gnats whirl in the air,
  The evening gnats, and there
The owl opes broad his eyes and wings to sail
For prey ; the bat wakes ; and the shell-less snail
  Comes forth clammy and bare.

  Hark ! that's the nightingale,
  Telling the self-same tale
Her song told when this ancient earth was young ;
So echoes answered when her song was sung
  In the first wooded vale.

  We call it love and pain
  The passion of her strain ;
And yet we little understand or know :
Why should it not be rather joy that so
  Throbs in each throbbing vein ?

  In separate herds the deer
  Lie ; here the bucks, and here
The does, and by its mother sleeps the fawn :
Through all the hours of night until the dawn
  They sleep, forgetting fear.

The hare sleeps where it lies
With wary half-closed eyes;
The cock has ceased to crow, the hen to cluck:
Only the fox is out, some heedless duck
Or chicken to surprise.

Remote, each single star
Comes out, till there they are
All shining brightly: how the dews fall damp!
While close at hand the glowworm lights her lamp
Or twinkles from afar.

But evening now is done
As much as if the sun
Day-giving had arisen in the east:
For night has come, and the great calm has ceased,
The quiet sands have run.

Christina Rossetti.

A SUMMER EVE.

DOWN the sultry arc of day
The burning wheels have urged their way,
And Eve along the western skies,
Spreads her intermingling dyes,

Down the deep, the miry lane,
Creeking comes the empty wain,
And driver on the shaft-horse sits,
Whistling now and then by fits;
And oft with his accustom'd call,
Urging on the sluggish Ball.
The barn is still, the master's gone,
And thresher puts his jacket on,
While Dick, upon the ladder tall,
Nails the dead kite to the wall.
Here comes shepherd Jack at last,
He has penn'd the sheep-cote fast,
For 'twas but two nights before
A lamb was eaten on the moor:
His empty wallet *Rover* carries,
Now for Jack, when near home, tarries;
With lolling tongue he runs to try,
If the horse-trough be not dry.
The milk is settled in the pans,
And supper messes in the cans;
In the hovel carts are wheel'd,
And both the colts are drove a-field;
The horses are all bedded up,
And the ewe is with the tup,
The snare for Mister Fox is set,
The leaven laid, the thatching wet,
And Bess has slinked away to talk
With Roger in the holly-walk.

Now on the settle all, but Bess,
Are set to eat their supper mess:
And little Tom and roguish Kate
Are swinging on the meadow gate.
Now they chat of various things,
Of taxes, ministers, and kings,
Or else tell all the village news,
How madam did the squire refuse;

Darjou pinx.^t   Pirodon Lith

How parson on his tithes was bent,
And landlord oft distrain'd for rent.
Thus do they talk, till in the sky
The pale-eyed moon is mounted high,
And from the alehouse drunken Ned
Has reel'd—then hasten all to bed.
The mistress sees that lazy Kate
The happing coal on kitchen grate
Has laid—while master goes throughout,
Sees shutters fast, the mastiff out,
The candles safe, the hearths all clear,
And nought from thieves or fire to fear,
Then both to bed together creep,
And join the general troop of sleep.

                         H. Kirke White.

EVENING.

FROM yonder wood mark blue-eyed Eve proceed:
First thro' the deep and warm and secret glens,
Through the pale glimmering privet-scented lane,
And through those alders by the river-side:
Now the soft dust impedes her, which the sheep
Have hollow'd out beneath their hawthorn shade.
But ah! look yonder! see a misty tide
Rise up the hill, lay low the frowning grove,
Enwrap the gay white mansion, sap its sides
Until they sink and melt away like chalk;
Now it comes down against our village-tower,
Covers its base, floats o'er its arches, tears

The clinging ivy from the battlements,
Mingles in broad embrace the obdurate stone,
(All one vast ocean), and goes swelling on
In slow and silent, dim and deepening waves.

W. S. Landor.

THE NIGHTS.

H the summer night
   Has a smile of light
And she sits on a sapphire throne ;
   Whilst the sweet winds load her
   With garlands of odour,
From the bud to the rose o'er blown !

   But the autumn night
   Has a piercing sight, •
   And a step both strong and free ;
   And a voice for wonder,
   Like the wrath of the thunder,
When he shouts to the stormy sea !

   And the winter night
   Is all cold and white,
And she singeth a song of pain ;
   Till the wild bee hummeth,
   And warm spring cometh,
When she dies in a dream of rain !

   O the night brings sleep
   To the green woods deep ;
To the bird of the woods its nest ;
   To care soft hours ;
   To life new powers ;
To the sick and the weary—Rest !

Barry Cornwall.

THE JACKDAW.

THERE is a bird, who, by his coat,
And by the hoarseness of his note,
 Might be supposed a crow ;
A great frequenter of the church,
Where, bishop-like, he finds a perch,
 And dormitory too.

Above the steeple shines a plate,
That turns and turns, to indicate
 From what point blows the weather,
Look up—your brains begin to swim,
'Tis in the clouds—that pleases him,
 He chooses it the rather.

Fond of the speculative height,
Thither he wings his airy flight,
 And thence securely sees
The bustle and the raree-show
That occupy mankind below,
Secure, and at his ease.

You think, no doubt, he sits and muses
On future broken bones and bruises,
 If he should chance to fall.
No ; not a single thought like that
Employs his philosophic pate,
 Or troubles it at all.

He see, that this great roundabout,
The world, with all its motley rout,
 Church, army, physic, law,
Its customs and its businesses
Is no' concern at all of his,
 And says—what says he ?—Caw.

Thrice-happy bird! I too have seen
Much of the vanities of men;
   And sick of having seen 'em,
Would cheerfully these limbs resign
For such a pair of wings as thine,
   And such a head between 'em.

                     W. Cowper.

THE THRUSH.

'LL pay my rent in music,' said a thrush,
Who took his lodging 'neath my eaves in
   spring,
Where the thick foliage droop'd. And well
   he kept
His simple contract. Not for quarter-day
He coldly waited, nor a draft required
To stir his memory, nor my patience tried
With changeful currencies, but every morn
Brought me good notes at par, and broke my
   sleep
With his sweet-ringing coin.

           Sometimes a song,
All wildly trilling through his dulcet pipes,
Falling, and caught again, and still prolong'd,—
Betrayed in what green nook the warbler sat,
Each feather quivering with excess of joy,
While from his opening beak and brightening eye
There seem'd to breathe a cadence, 'This is meant
For your especial benefit.' The lay
With overruling shrillness more than once
Did summon me to lay my book aside
And wait its close; nor was that pause a loss,

But seemed to tune and shape the inward ear
To wisdom's key-tone.

        Then I had a share
In softer songs, that cheer'd his brooding mate,
Who, in the patience of good hope, did keep
Her lengthen'd vigil; and the voice of love
That flow'd so fondly from his trusting soul
Made glad mine own.

        Then, too, there was a strain
From blended throats, that to their callow young
Breathed tenderness untold; and the weak chirp
Of new-born choristers, so deftly train'd
Each in the sweet way that he ought to go,
Mix'd with that breath of household charities
Which makes the spirit strong.

        And so I felt
My rent was fully paid, and thought myself
Quite fortunate, in these our times, to find
Such honest tenant.

        But when autumn bade
The northern birds to spread their parting wing,
And that small house was vacant, and o'er hedge
And russet grove and forest hoar with years
The hush of silence settled, I grew sad
To miss my kind musicians, and was fain
To patronize with a more fervent zeal
Such fireside music as makes winter short,
And storms unheard.

        Yet leave within our hearts
Dear melodists, the spirit of your praise;
Until ye come again; and the brown nest,
That now its downy lining to the winds

II

Turns desolate, shall thrill at your return
With the loud welcome home.

For He who touch'd
Your breasts with minstrelsy, and every flower
With beauty, hath a lesson for his sons,
In all the varied garniture that decks
Life's banquet-board; and he's the wisest guest
Who taketh gladly what his God doth send,
Keeping each instrument of joy in tune
That helps to fit him for the choir of heaven.

Mrs. Sigourney.

THE SWANS.

HUSH! my heedless feet from under
   Slip the crumbling banks for ever;
Like echoes to a distant thunder,
   They plunge into the gentle river.
The river-swans have heard my tread,
And startle from their reedy bed.

O beauteous birds! methinks ye measure
   Your movements to some heavenly tune!
O beauteous birds! 'tis such a pleasure
   To see you move beneath the moon,
I would it were your true delight
To sleep by day and wake all night.

S. T. Coleridge.

THE BELFRY PIGEON.

On the cross-beam under the old south bell
The nest of a pigeon is builded well.
In summer and winter that bird is there,
Out and in with the morning air:
I love to see him track the street,
With his wary eye and active feet;
And I often watch him as he springs,
Circling the steeple with easy wings,
Till across the dial his shade has pass'd,
And the belfry edge is gain'd at last.

'Tis a bird I love, with its brooding note,
And the trembling throb in its mottled throat;
There's a human look in its swelling breast,
And the gentle curve of its lowly crest;
And I often stop with the fear I feel—
He runs so close to the rapid wheel.

Whatever is rung on that noisy bell—
Chime of the hour or funeral knell—
The dove in the belfry must hear it well,
When the tongue swings out to the midnight moon—

When the sexton cheerly rings for noon—
When the clock strikes clear at morning light—
When the child is waked with "nine at night"-
When the chimes play soft in the Sabbath air,
Filling the spirit with tones of prayer—
Whatever and all in the bell is heard,
He broods on his folded feet unstirr'd,
Or, rising half in his rounded nest,
He takes the time to smooth his breast,
Then drops again with filmed eyes,
And sleeps as the last vibration dies.

Sweet bird! I would that I could be
A hermit in the crowd like thee!
With wings to fly to wood and glen,
Thy lot, like mine, is cast with men,
And daily, with unwilling feet,
Tread, like thee, the crowded street;
But, unlike me, when day is o'er,
Thou canst dismiss the world and soar,
Or, at a half-felt wish for rest,
Canst smooth the feathers on thy breast,
And drop, forgetful, to thy nest.

N. P. Willis.

THE OWL.

Aloft in my ancient, sky-roofed hall,
  In my old gray turret high,
Where the ivy waves o'er the crumbling wall,
  A king! a king reign I!
      Tu-whoo!
I wake the woods with my startling call
  To the frighted passer-by.

The gadding vines in the chinks that grow
  Come clambering up to me;
And the newt, the bat, and the toad, I trow,
  A merry band are we.
      Tu-whoo!
Oh! the coffined monks in their cells below,
  Have no goodlier company.

When the sweet dew sleeps in the midnight cool,
  To some tree-top I win;
While the toad leaps up on her throne-like stool,
  And our revels loud begin—
      Tu-whoo!
And the bull-frog croaks by yon stagnant pool,
  Ere he sportive plunges in.

And the blind bat wheels through the cloister shades,
    Where none unscared may pass;
And the newt glides forth through the long arcades,
    Where the glowworm lights the grass—
        Tu-whoo!
And will-o'-the-wisp, o'er the broad green glades,
    Flits on to the far morass.

And thus I ween all the livelong night
    A gladsome life lead we;
While the stars look down from their jewelled height
    On our sports approvingly.
        Tu-whoo!
They may bask who will in the mid-day light.
    But the midnight gloom for me!

                    Mary E. Howitt.

TO THE GRASSHOPPER AND THE CRICKET.

GREEN little vaulter in the sunny grass,
Catching your heart up at the feel of June,
Sole voice that's heard amidst the lazy noon,
When even the bees lag at the summoning brass;
And you, warm little housekeeper, who class
With those who think the candles come too soon,
Loving the fire, and with your tricksome tune
Nick the glad silent moments as they pass;

O sweet and tiny cousins, that belong,
One to the fields, the other to the hearth!
Both have your sunshine; both, though small, are strong,
At your clear hearts, and both seem given to earth
To ring in thoughtful ears this natural song—
In doors and out, summer and winter, mirth.

                    Leigh Hunt.

THE GRASSHOPPER AND THE CRICKET.

THE poetry of earth is never dead:
 When all the birds are faint with the hot sun,
 And hide in cooling trees, a voice will run
From hedge to hedge about the new-mown mead:
That is the grasshopper's—he takes the lead
 In summer luxury—he has never done
 With his delights, for when tired out with fun,
He rests at ease beneath some pleasant weed.
The poetry of earth is ceasing never:
 On a lone winter evening, when the frost
Has wrought a silence, from the stove there shrills
The cricket's song, in warmth increasing ever,
 And seems to one, in drowsiness half lost,
The grasshopper's among some grassy hills.

       J. Keats.

THE BEE.

THOU wert out betimes, thou busy, busy bee!
 As abroad I took my early way,
Before the cow from her resting-place
 Had risen up and left her trace
On the meadow, with dew so gray,
 Saw I thee, thou busy, busy bee.

Thou wert working late, thou busy, busy bee!
 After the fall of the cistus flower,
When the primrose-of-evening was ready to burst,
 I heard thee last, as I saw thee first;
In the silence of the evening hour,
 Heard I thee, thou busy, busy bee.

Thou art a miser, thou busy, busy bee!
  Late and early at employ;
Still on thy golden stores intent,
  Thy summer in heaping and hoarding is spent,
What thy winter will never enjoy;
  Wise lesson this for me, thou busy, busy bee!

Little dost thou think, thou busy, busy bee!
  What is the end of thy toil.
When the latest flowers of the ivy are gone,
  And all thy work for the year is done,
Thy master comes for the spoil.
  Woe then for thee, thou busy, busy bee!

R. Southey.

BEES.

THEREFORE doth Heaven divide
The state of man in divers functions,
Setting endeavour in continual motion;
To which is fixed, as an aim or butt,
Obedience: for so work the honey-bees;
Creatures, that, by a rule in nature, teach
The act of order to a peopled kingdom.
They have a king and officers of sorts:
Where some, like magistrates, correct at home;
Others, like merchants, venture trade abroad;
Others, like soldiers, armëd in their stings,
Make boot upon the summer's velvet buds;
Which pillage they with merry march bring home
To the tent-royal of their emperor:
Who, busied in his majesty, surveys
The singing masons building roofs of gold;
The civil citizens kneading up the honey;

The poor mechanic porters crowding in
Their heavy burthens at his narrow gate;
The sad-eyed justice, with his surly hum,
Delivering o'er to executors pale
The lazy yawning drone.

W. Shakspere.

THE GLOWWORM.

BENEATH the hedge, or near the stream,
  A worm is known to stray;
That shows by night a lucid beam
  Which disappears by day.

Disputes have been, and still prevail,
  From whence his rays proceed;
Some give that honour to his tail,
  And others to his head.

But this is sure—the hand of night
  That kindles up the skies,
Gives him a modicum of light,
  Proportion'd to his size.

Perhaps indulgent Nature meant,
  By such a lamp bestow'd,
To bid the traveller, as he went,
  Be careful where he trod;

Nor crush a worm, whose useful light
  Might serve, however small,
To show a stumbling-stone by night,
  And save him from a fall.

Whate'er she meant, this truth divine
  Is legible and plain,
'Tis power almighty bids him shine,
  Nor bids him shine in vain.

I

Ye proud and wealthy, let this theme
  Teach humbler thoughts to you,
Since such a reptile has its gem,
  And boasts its splendour too.

W. Cowper.

THE HEDGE-ROWS.

BEHOLD—a length of hundred leagues displayed—
That web of old historic tapestry
With its green patterns, broidered to the eye,
Is with domestic mysteries inlaid!
Here hath a nameless sire in some past age
In quaint uneven stripe or curious nook,
Clipped by the wanderings of a snaky brook,
Carved for a younger son an heritage.
There set apart, an island in a bower,
With right of road among the oakwoods round,
Are some few fields within a ring-fence bound,
Perchance a daughter's patrimonial dower.

So may we dream, while to our fancy come
Kind incidents and sweet biographies,
Scarce fanciful, as flowing from the ties
And blissful bonds which consecrate our home
To be an earthly heaven. From shore to shore
That ample, wind-stirred network doth ensnare
Within its delicate meshes many a rare
And rustic legend, which may yield good store
Of touching thought unto the passenger:
Domestic changes, families decayed,
And love or hate, in testaments displayed
By dying men, still in the hedge-rows stir.

F. W. Faber.

FIELD FLOWERS.

Yᴇ field flowers! the gardens eclipse you, 'tis true,
Yet, wildings of Nature, I doat upon you,
    For ye waft me to summers of old,
When the earth teem'd around me with fairy delight,
And when daisies and buttercups gladdened my sight,
    Like treasures of silver and gold.

I love you for lulling me back into dreams
Of the blue Highland mountains and echoing streams,
    And of birchen glades breathing their balm,
While the deer was seen glancing in sunshine remote,
And the deep mellow crush of the wood-pigeon's note
    Made music that sweeten'd the calm.

Not a pastoral song has a pleasanter tune
Than ye speak to my heart, little wildings of June :
    Of old ruinous castles ye tell,
Where I thought it delightful your beauties to find,
When the magic of Nature first breath'd on my mind,
    And your blossoms were part of her spell.

Even now what affections the violet awakes ;
What loved little islands, twice seen in their lakes,
    Can the wild water-lily restore ;
What landscapes I read in the primrose's looks,
And what pictures of pebbled and minnowy brooks,
    In the vetches that tangled their shore !

Earth's cultureless buds, to my heart ye were dear,
Ere the fever of passion or ague of fear
    Had scathed my existence's bloom ;
Once I welcome you more, in life's passionless stage,
With the visions of youth to revisit my age,
    And I wish you to grow on my tomb.

T. Campbell.

THE DAISY.

WITH little here to do or see
Of things that in the great world be,
Daisy ! again I talk to thee,
    ,   For thou art worthy.
Thou unassuming commonplace
Of Nature, with that homely face,
And yet with something of a grace,
    Which Love makes for thee !

Oft on the dappled turf at ease
I sit and play with similes,
Loose types of things through all degrees,
    Thoughts of thy raising:
And many a fond and idle name
I give to thee for praise or blame,
As is the humour of the game,
    While I am gazing.

A nun demure of lowly port;
Or sprightly maiden of Love's court,
In thy simplicity the sport
    Of all temptations;
A queen in crown of rubies drest;
A starveling in a scanty vest;
Are all, as seems to suit thee best,
    Thy appellations.

A little cyclops, with one eye
Staring to threaten and defy,
That thought comes next—and instantly
    The freak is over,
The shape will vanish—and behold
A silver shield with boss of gold,
That spreads itself, some fairy bold
    In fight to cover!

I see thee glittering from afar—
And then thou art a pretty star;
Not quite so fair as many are
    In heaven above thee!
Yet like a star, with glittering crest,
Self-poised in air thou seem'st to rest;—
May peace come never to his nest,
    Who shall reprove thee!

Bright *Flower!* for by that name at last,
When all my reveries are past,
I call thee, and to that cleave fast,
  Sweet silent creature!
That breath'st with me in sun and air,
Do thou, as thou art wont, repair
My heart with gladness, and a share
  Of thy meek nature!

  W. Wordsworth.

THE

DANDELION.

EAR common flower, that grow'st beside the way,
  Fringing the dusty road with harmless gold,
    First pledge of blithesome May,
  Which children pluck, and full of pride, uphold,
High-hearted buccaneers, o'erjoyed that they
An Eldorado in the grass have found,
  Which not the rich earth's ample round
May match in wealth,—thou art more dear to me
Than all the prouder summer blooms may be.

Gold such as thine ne'er drew the Spanish prow
Through the primeval hush of Indian seas,
  Nor wrinkled the lean brow
Of age, to rob the lover's heart of ease;
  'Tis the Spring's largess, which she scatters now

To rich and poor alike, with lavish hand ;
   Though most hearts never understand
   To take it at God's value, but pass by
   The offered wealth with unrewarded eye.

   Thou art my tropics and mine Italy ;
To look on thee unlocks a warmer clime ;
     The eyes thou givest me
Are in the heart, and heed not space or time :
   Not in mid June the golden-cuirassed bee
Feels a more summer-like, warm ravishment
     In the white lily's breezy tent,
   His conquered Sybaris, than I, when first
From the dark green thy yellow circles burst.

   Then think I of deep shadows on the grass,—
Of meadows where in sun the cattle graze,
     Where, as the breezes pass
The gleaming rushes lean a thousand ways,—
   Of leaves that slumber in a cloudy mass,
Or whiten in the wind,—of waters blue
     That from the distance sparkle through
   Some woodland gap,—and of a sky above,
   Where one white cloud like a stray lamb doth move.

   My childhood's earliest thoughts are linked with thee ;
The sight of thee calls back the robin's song,
     Who, from the dark old tree
Beside the door, sang clearly all day long,
   And I, secure in childish piety,
Listened as if I heard an angel sing
     With news from heaven, which he did bring
   Fresh every day to my untainted ears
   When birds and flowers and I were happy peers.

   How like a prodigal doth nature seem,
When thou, for all thy gold, so common art !
     Thou teachest me to deem
More sacredly of every human heart,
   Since each reflects in joy its scanty gleam

Of heaven, and could some wondrous secret show,
  Did we but pay the love we owe,
And with a child's undoubting wisdom look
On all these living pages of God's book.

J. R. Lowell.

THE SWEETBRIAR.

WILD rose, sweetbriar, eglantine,
All these pretty names are mine,
And scent in every leaf is mine,
And a leaf for all is mine,
And the scent—oh, that's divine!
Happy-sweet and pungent-fine,
Pure as dew, and pick'd as wine.

As the rose in gardens dress'd
Is the lady self-possess'd;
I'm the lass in simple vest,
The country lass whose blood's the best.
Were the beams that thread the briar
In the morn with golden fire
Scented, too, they'd smell like me,
All Elysian pungency.

Leigh Hunt.

THE GARDEN.

DEAR garden! once again with lingering look
Reverted, half remorseful, let me dwell
Upon thee as thou wert in that old time
Of happy days departed. Thou art changed,

And I have changed thee—Was it wisely done?
Wisely and well, they say who look thereon
With unimpassioned eye—cool, clear, undimm'd
By moisture such as memory gathers oft
In mine, while gazing on the things that are
Not with the hallowed past, the loved the lost
Associated as those I now retrace
With tender sadness. The old shrubbery walk
Straight as an arrow, was less graceful far
Than this fair winding among flowers and turf,
Till with an artful curve it sweeps from sight
To reappear again, just seen and lost
Among the hawthorns in the little dell.
Less lovely the old walk, but there I ran
Holding my mother's hand, a happy child;
There were her steps imprinted, and my father's,
And those of many a loved one, now laid low
In his last resting place. No flowers, methinks,
That now I cultivate are half so sweet,
So bright, so beautiful as those that bloomed
In the old formal borders. These clove pinks
Yield not such fragrance as the true old sort
That spiced our pot-pourrie (my mother's pride)
With such peculiar richness; and this rose,
With its fine foreign name, is scentless, pale,
Compared with the old cabbage—those that blushed
In the thick hedge of spiky lavender—
Such lavender as is not now-a-days;
And gilly-flowers are not as they were then
Sure to "come double;" and the night breeze now
Sighs not so loaded with delicious scents
Of lily and sevinger. O, my heart!
Is all indeed so altered?—or art thou
The changeling, sore aweary now at times
Of all beneath the sun?

Caroline Southey.

K

THE FOUNTAIN.

Into the sunshine, full of the light,
Leaping and flashing from morn till night!

Into the moonlight, whiter than snow,
Waving so flower-like when the winds blow!

Into the starlight, rushing in spray,
Happy at midnight, happy by day!

Ever in motion, blithesome and cheery,
Still climbing heavenward, never aweary ;—

Glad of all weathers, still seeming best,
Upward or downward, motion thy rest ;—

Full of a nature nothing can tame
Changed every moment, ever the same ;

Ceaseless aspiring, ceaseless content,
Darkness or sunshine thy element ;

Glorious fountain ! Let my heart be
Fresh, changeful, constant, upward, like thee !

J. R. Lowell.

THE COTTAGE.

MINE be a cot beside the hill ;
  A beehive's hum shall soothe my ear ;
A willowy brook that turns a mill,
  With many a fall shall linger near.

The swallow, oft, beneath my thatch
  Shall twitter from her clay-built nest ;
Oft shall the pilgrim lift the latch,
  And share my meal, a welcome guest.

Around my ivied porch shall spring
  Each fragrant flower that drinks the dew ;
And, Lucy, at her wheel, shall sing
  In russet-gown and apron blue.

The village church among the trees,
  Where first our marriage vows were given,
With merry peals shall swell the breeze,
  And point with taper spire to Heaven.

S. Rogers.

HAY MIAKEN.

'Tis merry ov a zummer's day,
Wher vo'ke be out a-miakèn hây;
Wher men an' women in a string
Da ted ar turn the grass, an' zing,

Wi' cheemen vâices, merry zongs,
A-tossèn o' ther sheenen prongs
Wi' yarms a-zwangèn left an' right,
In colour'd gowns an' shirt sleeves white;
Ar, wider spread, a-riakèn roun'
The ruosy hedges o' the groun'
Wher Sam da zee the speckled sniake,
An' try to kill en wi' his riake;
An' Poll da jump about an' squâl,
To zee the twistèn slooworm crâl.

'Tis merry wher a gây-tongued lot
Ov hây-miakers be all a-squot,
On lightly-russlèn hây a-spread
Below an elem's lofty head,
To rest ther weary limbs an' munch
Ther bit o' dinner, ar ther nunch;
Wher teethy riakes da lie all roun'
By picks a-stuck up into groun':
An' wi' ther vittles in ther laps,
An' in ther tinnen cups ther draps
O' cider sweet, ar frothy yale,
Ther tongues da run wi' joke an' tiale.

An' when the zun, so low an' red,
Da sheen above the leafy head
O' zome girt tree, a rizèn high
Avore the vi'ry western sky,
'Tis merry wher all han's da goo
Adirt the groun', by two an' two,
A-riakèn, anver humps an' hollers,
The russlèn grass up into rollers.

An' oone da row it in in line,
An' oone da cluose it up behine ;
An' ā'ter they the little buoys
Da stride an' fling ther yarms all woys,
Wi' busy picks an' proud young looks
A-miakèn up ther tiny pooks.
An' zoo 'tis merry out among
The vo'ke in hây-viel' al da-long.

William Barnes.

A GIPSY ENCAMPMENT.

SEE a column of slow-rising smoke
O'ertop the lofty wood that skirts the wild :
A vagabond and useless tribe there eat
Their miserable meal. A kettle, slung
Between two poles upon a stick transverse,
Receives the morsel—flesh obscene of dog,
Or vermin, or at best of cock purloined
From his accustomed perch. Hard-faring race !
They pick their fuel out of every hedge,
Which, kindled with dry leaves, just saves unquench'd
The spark of life. The sportive wind blows wide
Their fluttering rags, and shows a tawny skin,
The vellum of the pedigree they claim.
Great skill have they in palmistry, and more
To conjure clean away the gold they touch,
Conveying worthless dross into its place ;
Loud when they beg, dumb only when they steal.
Strange ! that a creature, rational, and cast
In human mould, should brutalize by choice
His nature ; and, though capable of arts
By which the world might profit, and himself,
Self-banished from society, prefer
Such squalid sloth to honourable toil !

Yet even these, though feigning sickness oft
They swathe the forehead, drag the limping limb,
And vex their flesh with artificial sores,
Can change their whine into a mirthful note,
When safe occasion offers; and with dance
And music of the bladder and the bag,
Beguile their woes, and make the woods resound.
Such health and gaiety of heart enjoy
The houseless rovers of the sylvan world;
And, breathing wholesome air, and wandering much,
Need other physic none to heal the effects
Of loathsome diet, penury, and cold.

W. Cowper.

ANGLING.

FLOW, river, flow!
Where the alders grow;—
Where the mosses rest
On the bank's high breast;
Flow on, and make sweet music ever,
Thou joyous and beloved river.

Such peace upon the landscape broods,
There is such beauty in the woods;
Such notes of joy come from the copse,
And from the swinging oak-tree tops;
There are such sounds of life, and health, and pleasure
    Abroad upon the breeze,
And on the river rippling at sweet leisure,
    Beneath its banks of fringing trees,—
That to my mind a thought of death or pain
Seems a discordant note in heavenly strain.

Death is the rule of life: the hawk in air
Pursues the swallow for his daily fare;

The blackbird and the linnet rove
On a death-errand through the grove;
The happy slug and glowworm pale,
Must die to feed the nightingale;
The mighty lion hunts his destined prey;
And the small insect, fluttering on our way,

Devours the tinier tribes that live unseen
In shady nooks and populous forests green;
The hungry fish, in seas and rivers,
Are death-receivers and death-givers;
And animalculæ conceal'd from sight,
In littleness sublime and infinite,
That whirl in drops of water from the fen—
Creatures as quarrelsome as men—
Or float in air upon invisible wings,
Devour the countless hosts of smaller things.
But simple is the law which they obey—
They never torture when they slay,
Unconquerable need, the law of life,
Impels the fiercest to the fatal strife:
They feel no joy in stopping meaner breath,
'Tis man alone that makes a sport of death.

So, gentle river, flow,
Where the green alders grow,

Where the pine-tree rears its crest,
And the stock-dove builds her nest,
Where the wild-flower odours float,
And the lark with gushing throat
Pours out her rapturous strains
To all hills and plains;
And if, amid the stream,
The lurking angler dream,
Of hooking fishes with his treacherous flies,
Reflect, oh river, the unclouded skies,
And bear no windy ripple on thy breast,—
The cloud and ripple he loves best,—
So that the innocent fish may see,
And shun their biped enemy.

Flow, river, flow,
Where the violets grow,
Where the bank is steep,
And the mosses sleep,
And the green trees nod to thy waves below:
Flow on and make sweet music ever,
Thou joyous and beloved river!

                              C. Mackay.

THE DESOLATE VILLAGE.

I WALKED by mysel' ower the sweet braes o' Yarrow,
    When the earth wi' the gowans o' July was drest;
But the sang o' the bonny burn sounded like sorrow,
    Round ilka house cauld as a last simmer's nest.

I look'd through the lift o' the blue smiling morning,
    But never ae wee cloud o' mist could I see
On its way up to heaven, the cottage adorning,
    Hanging white ower the green o' its sheltering tree.

By the outside I kenn'd that the inner was forsaken,
  That nae tread o' footsteps was heard on the floor;
O loud craw'd the cock whare was nane to awaken,
  And the wild raven croak'd on the seat by the door!

Sic silence—sic lonesomeness, oh, were bewildering!
  I heard nae lass singing when herding her sheep;
I met nae bright garlands o' wee rosy children
  Dancing on to the schoolhouse just waken'd frae sleep.

I pass'd by the school-house—when strangers were coming,
  Whase windows with glad faces seem'd all alive;
Ae moment I hearken'd, but heard nae sweet humming,
  For a night o' dark vapour can silence the hive.

I pass'd by the pool where the lasses at daw'ing
  Used to bleach their white garments wi' daffin and din;
But the foam in the silence o' nature was fa'ing,
  And nae laughing rose loud through the roar of the linn.

I gaed into a small town—when sick o' my roaming—
  Whare ance play'd the viol, the tabor, and flute;
'Twas the hour loved by labour, the saft smiling gloaming,
  Yet the green round the Cross-stane was empty and mute.

To the yellow-flower'd meadow, and scant rigs o' tillage,
  The sheep a' neglected had come frae the glen;
The cushat-dow coo'd in the midst o' the village;
  And the swallow had flown to the dwellings of men!

Sweet Denholm! not thus, when I lived in thy bosom,
  Thy heart lay so still the last night o' the week;
Then nane was sae weary that love would nae rouse him,
  And grief gaed to dance with a laugh on his cheek.

Sic thoughts wet my een—as the moonshine was beaming
  On the kirk-tower that rose up sae silent and white;
The wan ghastly light on the dial was streaming,
  But the still finger tauld not the hour of the night.

L.

The mirk-time pass'd slowly in siching and weeping,
    I waken'd, and nature lay silent in mirth;
Ower a' holy Scotland the Sabbath was sleeping,
    And heaven in beauty came down on the earth.

The morning smiled on but nae kirk-bell was ringing,
    Nae plaid or blue bonnet came down frae the hill;
The kirk-door was shut, but nae psalm-tune was singing,
    And I miss'd the wee voices sae sweet and sae shrill.

I look'd ower the quiet o' Death's empty dwelling,
    The lav'rock walk'd mute 'mid the sorrowful scene,
And fifty brown hillocks wi' fresh mould were swelling
    Ower the kirk-yard o' Denholm, last summer sae green,

The infant had died at the breast o' its mither;
    The cradle stood still at the mitherless bed;
At play the bairn sunk in the hand o' its brither;
    At the fauld on the mountain the shepherd lay dead.

Oh! in spring-time 'tis eerie, when winter is over,
    And birds should be glinting ower forest and lea,
When the lintwhite and mavis the yellow leaves cover,
    And nae blackbird sings loud frae the tap o' his tree.

But eerier far, when the spring-land rejoices,
    And laughs back to heaven with gratitude bright;
To hearken! and naewhere hear sweet human voices,
    When man's soul is dark in the season o' light!

                                                J. Wilson.

SOLITUDE.

O VALE of visionary rest!
—Hush'd as the grave it lies
With heaving banks of tenderest green,
Yet brightly, happily serene,

As cloud-vale of the sleepy west
Reposing on the skies.
Its reigning spirit may not vary—
What change can seasons bring
Unto so sweet, so calm a spot,
Where every loud and restless thing
Is like a far-off dream forgot?
Mild, gentle, mournful, solitary,
As if it aye were spring,
And Nature lov'd to witness here,
The still joys of the infant year,
'Mid flowers and music wandering glad,
For ever happy, yet for ever sad.

This little world how still and lone
With that horizon of its own!
And, when in silence falls the night,
With its own moon how purely bright!
No shepherd's cot is here—no shealing
Its verdant roof through trees revealing—
No branchy covert like a nest,
Where the weary woodmen rest,
And their jocund carols sing
O'er the fallen forest-king.

Inviolate by human hand
The fragrant white-stemm'd birch-trees stand,
With many a green and sunny glade
'Mid their embowering murmurs made
By gradual soft decay—
Where stealing to that little lawn
From secret haunt and half afraid,
The doe, in mute affection gay,
At close of eve leads forth her fawn
Amid the flowers to play.
And in that dell's soft bosom, lo!
Where smileth up a cheerful glow
Of water pure as air,

A tarn by two small streamlets spread
In beauty o'er its waveless bed,
Reflecting in that heaven so still,
The birch-grove mid-way up the hill,
And summits green and bare.

How lone! beneath its veil of dew
That morning's rosy fingers drew,
Seldom shepherd's foot hath prest
One primrose in its sunny rest.
The sheep at distance from the spring
May here her lambkins chance to bring,
Sporting with their shadows airy,
Each like tiny water fairy
Imaged in the lucid lake!
The hive-bee here doth sometimes make
Music, whose sweet murmurings tell
Of his shelter'd straw-roof'd cell,
Standing 'mid some garden gay,
Near a cottage far away.
By the lake-side, on a stone
Stands the heron all alone,
Still as any lifeless thing!
Slowly moves his laggard wing,
And cloud-like floating with the gale
Leaves at last the quiet vale.

J. Wilson.

A MOUNTAIN STREAM.

THERE is a stream (I name not its name, lest inquisitive tourist
Hunt it, and make it a lion, and get it at last into guide-books)
Springing far off from a loch unexplored in the folds of great mountains,
Falling two miles through rowan and stunted alder, enveloped
Then for four more in a forest of pine, where broad and ample
Spreads, to convey it, the glen with heathery slopes on both sides:

Broad and fair the stream, with occasional falls and narrows ;
But, where the glen of its course approaches the vale of the river,
Met and blocked by a huge interposing mass of granite,
Scarce by a channel deep-cut, raging up, and raging onward,
Forces its flood through a passage so narrow a lady would step it.
There, across the great rocky wharves, a wooden bridge goes,
Carrying a path to the forest ; below, three hundred yards, say,
Lower in level some twenty-five feet, through flats of shingle,
Stepping-stones and a cart-track cross in the open valley.
But in the interval here the boiling pent-up water
Frees itself by a final descent, attaining a basin,
Ten feet wide and eighteen long, with whiteness and fury
Occupied partly, but mostly pellucid, pure, a mirror ;
Beautiful there for the colour derived from green rocks under ;
Beautiful, most of all, where beads of foam uprising
Mingle their clouds of white with the delicate hue of the stillness,
Cliff over cliff for its sides, with rowan and pendant birch boughs,
Here it lies, unthought of above at the bridge and pathway,
Still more enclosed from below by wood and rocky projection.
You are shut in, left alone with yourself and perfection of water,
Hid on all sides, left alone with yourself and the goddess of bathing.

A. H. Clough.

~~~~~~~~~~~~~~~~~~~~~~~~~~~

THE WIND.

THE wind went forth o'er land and sea,
Loud and free ;
Foaming waves leapt up to meet it,
Stately pines bowed down to greet it ;
While the wailing sea
And the forest's murmured sigh
Joined the cry
Of the wind that swept o'er land and sea.

The wind that blew upon the sea
                Fierce and free,
        Cast the bark upon the shore,
        Whence it sailed the night before
                Full of hope and glee;
And the cry of pain and death
                Was but a breath,
Through the wind that roared upon the sea.

The wind was whispering on the lea
                Tenderly;
        But the white rose felt it pass,
        And the fragile stalks of grass
                Shook with fear to see
All her trembling petals shed,
                As it fled
So gently by,—the wind upon the lea.

Blow, thou wind, upon the sea
                Fierce and free,
        And a gentler message send,
        Where frail flowers and grasses bend,
                On the sunny lea;
For thy bidding still is one,
                Be it done
In tenderness or wrath, on land or sea!

                              Adelaide A. Procter.

A SUMMER STORM.

UNTREMULOUS in the river clear,
Toward the sky's image, hangs the imaged bridge,
    So still the air, that I can hear
The slender clarion of the unseen midge;
    Out of the stillness, with a gathering creep,

Like rising wind in leaves, which now decreases,
Now lulls, now swells, and all the while increases,
  The huddling tramp of a drove of sheep,
Tilts the loose planks, and then as gradually ceases
  In dust on the other side; life's emblem deep,
A confused noise between two silences,
Finding at last in dust precarious peace.

On the wide marsh the purple-blossomed grasses
  Soak up the sunshine; sleeps the brimming tide,
Save when the wedge-shaped wake in silence passes
  Of some slow water-rat, whose sinuous glide
    Wavers the long green sedge's shade from side to side;
But up the west, like a rock-shivered surge,
  Climbs a great cloud edged with sun-whitened spray;
Huge whirls of foam boil toppling o'er its verge,
  And falling still it seems, and yet it climbs alway.

      Suddenly all the sky is hid
      As with the shutting of a lid,

One by one great drops are falling
 Doubtful and slow,
Down the pane they are crookedly crawling,
 And the wind breathes low;
Slowly the circles widen on the river,
 Widen and mingle, one and all;
Here and there the slenderer flowers shiver,
 Struck by an icy rain-drop's fall.

Now on the hills I hear the thunder mutter,
 The wind is gathering in the west;
The up-turned leaves first whiten and flutter,
 Then droop to a fitful rest;
Up from the stream with sluggish flap
 Struggles the gull, and floats away;
Nearer and nearer rolls the thunder-clap,—
 We shall not see the sun go down to-day:
Now leaps the wind on the sleepy marsh,
 And tramples the grass with terrified feet,
The startled river turns leaden and harsh,
 You can hear the quick heart of the tempest beat.

 Look! look! that livid flash!
And instantly follows the rattling thunder,
As if some cloud-crag, split asunder,
 Fell, splintering with a ruinous crash,
On the earth, which crouches in silence under;
 And now a solid gray wall of rain
Shuts off the landscape, mile by mile;
 For a breath's space I see the blue wood again,
And, ere the next heart-beat, the wind-hurled pile,
 That seemed but now a league aloof,
Bursts rattling over the sun-parched roof;

Against the windows the storm comes dashing,
Through tattered foliage the hail tears crashing,
 The blue lightning flashes
 The rapid hail clashes,
 The white waves are tumbling
  And; in one baffled roar,

Like the toothless sea mumbling
  A rock-bristled shore,
  The thunder is rumbling
  And crashing and crumbling,—
Will silence return never more ?

    Hush ! still as death,
    The tempest holds his breath
  As from a sudden will ;
The rain stops short, but from the eaves
You see it drop, and hear it from the leaves,
  All is so bodingly still ;
    Again, now, now, again
Plashes the rain in heavy gouts,
    The crinkled lightning
    Seems ever brightening,
      And loud and long
Again the thunder shouts
    His battle-song,—
    One quivering flash,
    One wildering crash,
  Followed by silence dead and dull,
    As if the cloud, let go,
    Leapt bodily below
To whelm the earth in one mad overthrow,
    And then a total lull.

    Gone, gone, so soon !
  No more my half-crazed fancy there
  Can shape a giant in the air,
  No more I see his streaming hair,
The writhing portent of his form ;—
    The pale and quiet moon
    Makes her calm forehead bare,
And the last fragments of the storm,
Like shattered rigging from a fight at sea,
Silent and few, are drifting over me.

                              J. R. Lowell.

M

THE CLOUD.

I bring fresh showers for the thirsting flowers,
　From the seas and the streams;
I bear light shades for the leaves when laid
　In their noon-day dreams.
From my wings are shaken the dews that waken
　The sweet buds every one,
When rocked to rest on their mother's breast,
　As she dances about the sun.
I wield the flail of the lashing hail,
　And whiten the green plains under,
And then again I dissolve in rain,
　And laugh as I pass in thunder.

I sift the snow on the mountains below,
　And their great pines groan aghast;
And all the night 'tis my pillow white,
　While I sleep in the arms of the blast.
Sublime on the towers of my skiey bowers,
　Lightning, my pilot, sits;
In a cavern under is fettered the thunder;
　It struggles and howls at fits:
Over earth and ocean, with gentle motion,
　This pilot is guiding me,
Lured by the love of the genii that move
　In the depths of the purple sea;
Over the rills, and the crags, and the hills,
　Over the lakes and the plains,
Wherever he dream, under mountain or stream,
　The spirit he loves remains;
And I all the while bask in heaven's blue smile,
　Whilst he is dissolving in rains.

The sanguine sunrise, with his meteor eyes,
　And his burning plumes outspread,
Leaps on the back of my sailing rack,
　When the morning star shines dead.

As on the jag of a mountain crag,
  Which an earthquake rocks and swings,
An eagle alit one moment may sit
  In the light of its golden wings.
And when sunset may breathe, from the lit sea beneath,
  Its ardours of rest and of love,
And the crimson pall of eve may fall
  From the depth of heaven above,
With wings folded I rest on mine airy nest,
  As still as a brooding dove.

That orbèd maiden, with white fire laden,
  Whom mortals call the Moon,
Glides glimmering o'er my fleece-like floor,
  By the midnight breezes strewn ;
And wherever the beat of her unseen feet,
  Which only the angels hear,
May have broken the woof of my tent's thin roof,
  The stars peep behind and peer ;
And I laugh to see them whirl and flee,
  Like a swarm of golden bees,
When I widen the rent in my wind-built tent,
  Till the calm rivers, lakes, and seas,
Like strips of the sky fallen through me on high,
  Are each paved with the moon and these.

I bind the sun's throne with the burning zone,
  And the moon's with a girdle of pearl ;
The volcanoes are dim, and the stars reel and swim,
  When the whirlwinds my banner unfurl.
From cape to cape, with a bridge-like shape,
  Over a torrent sea,
Sunbeam proof, I hang like a roof,
  The mountains its columns be.
The triumphal arch through which I march,
  With hurricane, fire, and snow,
When the powers of the air are chained to my chair,
  Is the million-coloured bow ;
The sphere-fire above its soft colours wove,
  While the moist earth was laughing below.

I am the daughter of earth and water,
  And the nursling of the sky:
I pass through the pores of the ocean and shores;
  I change, but I cannot die.
For after the rain, when with never a stain,
  The pavilion of heaven is bare,
And the winds and sunbeams, with their convex gleams,
  Build up the blue dome of air.
I silently laugh at my own cenotaph,
  And out of the caverns of rain,
Like a child from the womb, like a ghost from the tomb,
  I arise and unbuild it again.

                                        P. B. Shelley.

A RAILWAY JOURNEY.

THE young oak casts its delicate shadow
    Over the still and emerald meadow;
  The sheep are cropping the fresh spring grass,
    And never raise their heads as we pass;
  The cattle are taking their noon-day rest,
    And chewing the cud with a lazy zest,
  Or, bathing their feet in the reedy pool,
    Switch their tails in the shadows cool;
But away, away, we may not stay,
  Panting and puffing, and snorting and starting,
  And shrieking and crying, and madly flying,
On and on, there's a race to be run and a goal to be won ere
    the set of the sun.

Two white clouds are poised on high,
Sunning their wings in the azure sky;
Two white swans float to and fro
Languidly in the stream below,
As it sleeps beneath a beechwood tall,
Clouds, and swans, and trees, and all,

Image themselves in the quiet stream,
Passing their lives in a sunny dream;
But away, away, we may not stay,
Panting and puffing, and snorting and starting,
And shrieking and crying, and madly flying,
On and on, there's a race to be run and a goal to be won ere
the set of the sun.

Under the tall cliffs, green and deep,
The ocean rests in its mid-day sleep;
The waves are heaving lazily
Where the purple sea-weeds float;
Sunbeams cross on the distant sea,
Speck'd by the sail of the fisher's boat;
But away, away, we may not stay,
Panting and puffing, and snorting and starting,
And shrieking and crying, and madly flying,
On and on, there's a race to be run and a goal to be won ere
the set of the sun.

Into the deep dell's still retreat,
Where the river rushes beneath our feet,
Skirting the base of moorland hills,
By the side of rocky rills,

Where the wild-bird bathes and plumes its wing,
Where the fields are fresh with the breath of spring,
Where the earth is hush'd in her noon-day prayer,
No place so secret but we come there.
On nature's mid-day sleep we break,
And are miles away ere her echoes wake;
We startle the wood-nymphs in their play,
And ere they can hide are away, away!
 Away, away, we may not stay,
 Panting and puffing, and snorting and starting,
 And shrieking and crying, and madly flying,
On and on, there's a race to be run and a goal to be won ere
 the set of the sun.

     The Author of " The Three Wakings."

MOONLIGHT ON THE SEA.

It is the midnight hour:—the beauteous sea,
Calm as the cloudless heaven, the heaven discloses,
While many a sparkling star, in quiet glee,
Far down within the watery sky reposes.
As if the Ocean's heart were stirr'd
With inward life, a sound is heard,
Like that of dreamer murmuring in his sleep;
'Tis partly the billow, and partly the air
That lies like a garment floating fair
Above the happy deep.
The sea, I ween, cannot be fann'd
By evening freshness from the land,
For the land it is far away;
But God hath will'd that the sky-born breeze
In the centre of the loneliest seas
Should ever sport and play.
The mighty Moon she sits above,
Encircled with a zone of love,
A zone of dim and tender light,
That makes her wakeful eye more bright;

WOODCOCKS AND PLOVERS

She seems to shine with a sunny ray,
And the night looks like a mellow'd day!
The gracious Mistress of the Main
Hath now an undisturbed reign,
And from her silent throne looks down,
As upon children of her own,
On the waves that lend their gentle breast
In gladness for her couch of rest!
  My spirit sleeps amid the calm
The sleep of a new delight;
And hopes that she ne'er may awake again,
But for ever hang o'er the lovely main,
And adore the lovely night.
Scarce conscious of an earthly frame,
She glides away like a lambent flame,
And in her bliss she sings;
Now touching softly the ocean's breast,
Now mid the stars she lies at rest,
As if she sail'd on wings!
Now bold as the brightest star that glows
More brightly since at first it rose,
Looks down on the far-off flood,
And there all breathless and alone,
As the sky where she soars were a world of her own,
She mocketh that gentle mighty one
As he lies in his quiet mood.
"Art thou," she breathes, "the tyrant grim
That scoffs at human prayers,
Answering with prouder roar the while,
As it rises from some lonely isle
Through groans raised wild, the hopeless hymn
Of shipwreck'd mariners?
Oh! thou art harmless as a child
Weary with joy, and reconciled
For sleep to change its play;
And now that night hath stay'd thy race,
Smiles wander o'er thy placid face
As if thy dreams were gay."

J. Wilson.

THE SHORE.

TURN to the watery world!—but who to thee
  (A wonder yet unview'd) shall paint—the Sea?
Various and vast, sublime in all its forms,
  When lull'd by zephyrs, or when roused by storms,
    Its colours changing, when from clouds and sun
Shades after shades upon the surface run:
Embrown'd and horrid now, and now serene,
In limpid blue, and evanescent green;
And oft the foggy banks on ocean lie,
Lift the fair sail, and cheat the experienced eye.
  Be it the Summer-noon: a sandy space
The ebbing tide has left upon its place;
Then just the hot and stony beach above,
Light twinkling streams in bright confusion move;
(For heated thus, the warmer air ascends,
And with the cooler in its fall contends)—
Then the broad bosom of the ocean keeps
An equal motion, swelling as it sleeps,
Then slowly sinking; curling to the strand,
Faint, lazy waves o'ercreep the ridgy sand, .
Or tap the tarry boat with gentle blow,
And back return in silence, smooth and slow.

Ships in the calm seem anchor'd; for they glide
On the still sea, urged solely by the tide;
Art thou not present, this calm scene before,
Where all beside is pebbly length of shore,
And far as eye can reach, it can discern no more?
　Yet sometimes comes a ruffling cloud to make
The quiet surface of the ocean shake;
As an awaken'd giant with a frown
Might show his wrath, and then to sleep sink down.
　View now the Winter-storm! above, one cloud,
Black and unbroken, all the skies o'ershroud;
The unwieldy porpoise through the day before
Had roll'd in view of boding men on shore;
And sometimes hid and sometimes show'd his form,
Dark as the cloud, and furious as the storm.

All where the eye delights, yet dreads to roam,
The breaking billows cast the flying foam
Upon the billows rising—all the deep
Is restless change; the waves so swelled and steep,
Breaking and sinking, and the sunken swells,
Nor one, one moment, in its station dwells:
But nearer land, you may the billows trace,
As if contending in their watery chase;
May watch the mightiest till the shoal they reach,
Then break and hurry to their utmost stretch:
Curl'd as they come, they strike with furious force,
And then reflowing, take their grating course,
Raking the rounded flints, which ages past
Roll'd by their rage, and shall to ages last.
　Far off the petrel in the troubled way
Swims with her brood, or flutters in the spray;
She rises often, often drops again,
And sports at ease on the tempestuous main.
　High o'er the restless deep, above the reach
Of gunner's hope, vast flights of wild-ducks stretch;
Far as the eye can glance on either side,
In a broad space and level line they glide;

N

All in their wedge-like figures from the north,
Day after day, flight after flight, go forth.
  Inshore their passage tribes of sea-gulls urge;
And drop for prey within the sweeping surge;
Oft in the rough opposing blast they fly
Far back, then turn, and all their force apply,
While to the storm they give their weak complaining cry;
Or clap the sleek white pinion to the breast
And in the restless ocean dip for rest.

G. Crabbe.

A SEA-SIDE SONG.

The day is down into his bower:
  In languid lights his feet he steeps:
The flush'd sky darkens, low and lower,
  And closes on the glowing deeps.

In creeping curves of yellow foam
  Up shallow sands the waters slide:
And warmly blow what whispers roam
  From isle to isle the lullèd tide:

The boats are drawn: the nets drip bright:
  Dark casements gleam: old songs are sung:
And out upon the verge of night
  Green lights from lonely rocks are hung.

O winds of eve that somewhere rove
 Where darkest sleeps the distant sea,
Seek out where haply dreams my love,
 And whisper all her dreams to me!

Owen Meredith.

THE GREENWOOD.

'Tis merry in greenwood,—thus runs the old lay,—
In the gladsome month of lively May,
When the wild birds' song on stem and spray
 Invites to forest bower;
Then rears the ash his airy crest,
Then shines the birch in silver vest,
And the beech in glistening leaves is drest,
And dark between shows the oak's proud breast,
 Like a chieftain's frowning tower;
Though a thousand branches join their screen,
Yet the broken sunbeams glance between,
And tip the leaves with lighter green,
 With brighter tints the flower:
Dull is the heart that loves not then
The deep recess of the wild-wood glen,
Where roe and red-deer find sheltering den,
 When the sun is in his power.

Less merry, perchance, is the fading leaf
That follows so soon on the gather'd sheaf,
 When the greenwood loses the name;
Silent is then the forest bound,
Save the redbreast's note, and the rustling sound
Of frost-nipt leaves that are dropping round,
Or the deep-mouth'd cry of the distant hound
 That opens on his game:
Yet then, too, I love the forest wide,
Whether the sun in splendour ride,

And gild its many-colour'd side ;
Or whether the soft and silvery haze,
In vapoury folds, o'er the landscape strays,
And half involves the woodland maze ;
    Like an early widow's veil,
Where wimpling tissue from the gaze
The form half hides, and half betrays,
    Of beauty wan and pale.

                              Sir Walter Scott.

TO AUTUMN.

SEASON of mists and mellow fruitfulness !
    Close bosom-friend of the maturing sun ;
Conspiring with him how to load and bless
    With fruit the vines that round the thatch-eaves
      run ;
    To bend with apples the moss'd cottage-trees,
      And fill all fruit with ripeness to the core ;
      To swell the gourd, and plump the hazel shells
With a sweet kernel ; to set budding more,
And still more, later flowers for the bees,
Until they think warm days will never cease,
    For summer has o'er-brimm'd their clammy cells.

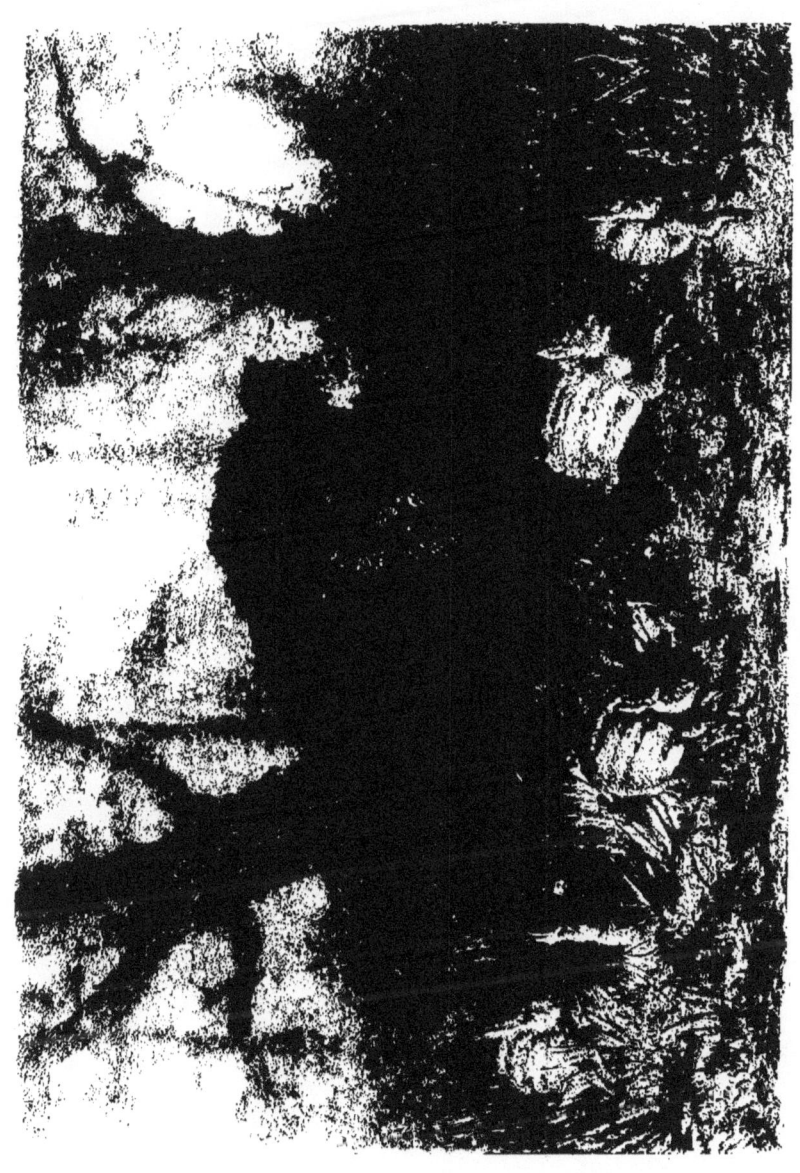

Who hath not seen thee oft amid thy store?
  Sometimes whoever seeks abroad may find
Thee sitting careless on a granary floor,
  Thy hair soft-lifted by the winnowing wind;
Or on a half-reap'd furrow sound asleep,
  Drowsed with the fume of poppies, while thy hook
    Spares the next swath and all its twinèd flowers;
And sometimes like a gleaner thou dost keep
  Steady thy laden head across a brook;
  Or by a cider-press, with patient look,
    Thou watchest the last oozings, hours by hours.

Where are the songs of spring? Ay, where are they?
  Think not of them, thou hast thy music too,
While barred clouds bloom the soft-dying day,
  And touch the stubble-plains with rosy hue;
Then in a wailful choir the small gnats mourn
  Among the river sallows, borne aloft
    Or sinking as the light wind lives or dies;
And full-grown lambs loud bleat from hilly bourn;
  Hedge-crickets sing: and now with treble soft
  The redbreast whistles from a garden-croft,
    And gathering swallows twitter in the skies.

John Keats.

AUTUMN.

Thou comest, Autumn, heralded by the rain,
With banners, by great gales incessant fanned,
Brighter than brightest silks of Samarcand,
And stately oxen harnessed to thy wain!
Thou standest, like imperial Charlemagne,
Upon thy bridge of gold; thy royal hand
Outstretched with benedictions o'er the land,
Blessing the farms through all thy vast domain.

Thy shield is the red harvest moon, suspended
So long beneath the heaven's o'erhanging eaves;
Thy steps are by the farmer's prayers attended;
Like flames upon an altar shine the sheaves;
And, following thee, in thy ovation splendid,
Thine almoner, the wind, scatters the golden leaves.

H. W. Longfellow.

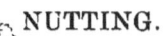

NUTTING.

——It seems a day
(I speak of one from many singled out),
One of those heavenly days that cannot die;
When, in the eagerness of boyish hope,
I left our cottage-threshold, sallying forth
With a huge wallet o'er my shoulders slung,
A nutting-crook in hand; and turned my steps
Tow'rd some far-distant wood, a figure quaint,
Trick'd out in proud disguise of cast-off weeds
Which for that service had been husbanded,
By exhortation of my frugal dame—
Motley accoutrement, of power to smile
At thorns, and brakes, and brambles,—and, in truth,
More ragged than need was! O'er pathless rocks,
Through beds of matted fern, and tangled thickets,
Forcing my way, I came to one dear nook
Unvisited, where not a broken bough
Drooped with its withered leaves, ungracious sign
Of devastation; but the hazels· rose
Tall and erect, with tempting clusters hung,
A virgin scene! A little while I stood,
Breathing with such suppression of the heart
As joy delights in; and, with wise restraint
Voluptuous, fearless of a rival, eyed
The banquet;—or beneath the trees I sate
Among the flowers, and with flowers I played;
A temper known to those, who, after long
And weary expectation, have been blest
With sudden happiness beyond all hope.
Perhaps it was a bower beneath whose leaves
The violets of five seasons re-appear
And fade, unseen by any human eye;
Where fairy water-breaks do murmur on
For ever; and I saw the sparkling foam,
And—with my cheek on one of those green stones

That, fleeced with moss, under the shady trees,
Lay round me, scattered like a flock of sheep—
I heard the murmur and the murmuring sound,
In that sweet mood when pleasure loves to pay
Tribute to ease ; and, of its joy secure,
The heart luxuriates with indifferent things,
Wasting its kindliness on stocks and stones
And on the vacant air. Then up I rose,
And dragged to earth both branch and bough with crash,
And merciless ravage : and the shady nook
Of hazels, and the green and mossy bower,
Deformed and sullied, patiently gave up
Their quiet being : and, unless I now
Confound my present feelings with the past,
Ere from the mutilated bower I turned
Exulting, rich beyond the wealth of kings,
I felt a sense of pain when I beheld
The silent trees, and saw the intruding sky.
Then, dearest maiden, move along these shades
In gentleness of heart; with gentle hand
Touch—for there is a spirit in the woods.

W. Wordsworth.

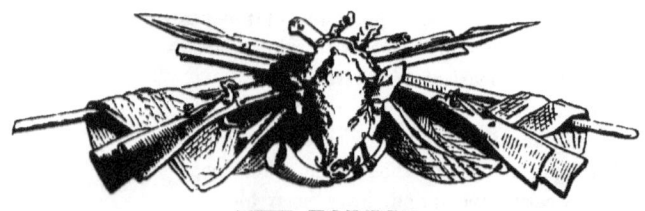

THE FOREST.

THE scenes are desert now and bare,
Where flourished once a forest fair,
When these waste glens with copse were lined,
And peopled with the hart and hind.
Yon thorn—perchance whose prickly spears
Have fenced him for three hundred years,

While fell around his green compeers—
Yon lonely thorn, would he could tell
The changes of his parent dell,

Since he, so gray and stubborn now,
Waved in each breeze a sapling bough ;
Would he could tell how deep the shade
A thousand mingled branches made,
How broad the shadows of the oak,
How clung the rowan to the rock,
And through the foliage showed his head,
With narrow leaves, and berries red ;
What pines on every mountain sprung,
O'er every dell what birches hung,
In every breeze what aspens shook,
What alders shaded every brook !

o

"Here, in my shade," methinks he'd say,
"The mighty stag at noontide lay:
The wolf I've seen, a fiercer game,
(The neighbouring dingle bears his name,)
With lurching step around me prowl,
And stop against the moon to howl;

The mountain boar, on battle set,
His tusks upon my stem would whet;
While doe and roe, and red-deer good,
Have bounded by through gay green-wood.
Then oft, from Newark's riven tower,
Sallied a Scottish monarch's power:
A thousand vassals mustered round,
With horse, and hawk, and horn, and hound;
And I might see the youth intent,
Guard every pass, with cross-bow bent;
And through the brake the rangers stalk,
And falconers hold the ready hawk;
And foresters, in green-wood trim,
Lead in the leash the gaze-hounds grim,
Attentive, as the bratchet's bay
From the dark covert drove the prey,
To slip them as he broke away.
The startled quarry bounds amain,
As fast the gallant greyhounds strain;
Whistles the arrow from the bow,

Answers the harquebuss below;
While all the rocking hills reply,
To hoof-clang, hound, and hunter's cry,
The bugles ringing lightsomely."

Sir Walter Scott.

COUNTRY SPORTS.

SEE! from the brake the whirring pheasant springs,
And mounts exulting on triumphant wings:
Short is his joy, he feels the fiery wound,
Flutters in blood, and panting beats the ground.
Ah! what avails his glossy, varying dyes,
His purple crest, and scarlet-circled eyes.
The vivid green his shining plumes unfold,
His painted wings, and breast that flames with gold?
  Nor yet, when moist Arcturus clouds the sky,
The woods and fields their pleasing toils deny.
To plains with well-breath'd beagles we repair,
And trace the mazes of the circling hare,
(Beasts, urged by us, their fellow-beasts pursue,
And learn of man each other to undo):
With slaughtering guns the unwearied fowler roves,
When frosts have whiten'd all the naked groves;
Where doves in flocks the leafless trees o'ershade,
And lonely woodcocks haunt the watery glade,
He lifts the tube, and levels with his eye:
Straight a short thunder breaks the frozen sky:

Oft, as in airy rings they skim the heath,
The clamorous lapwings feel the leaden death ;
Oft, as the mounting larks their notes prepare,
They .fail, and leave their little lives in air.

A. Pope.

SHOOTING.

HERE the rude clamour of the sportsman's. joy,
The gun fast thundering, and the winded horn,
Would tempt the muse to sing the rural game :
How, in his mid-career, the spaniel, struck
Stiff by the tainted gale, with open nose,
Outstretch'd, and finely sensible, draws full,
Fearful, and cautious, on the latent prey ;
As in the sun the circling covey bask
Their varied plumes, and watchful every way,
Through the rough stubble turn the secret eye,
Caught in the meshy snare, in vain they beat
Their idle wings, entangled more and more ;

Nor on the surges of the boundless air,
Though borne triumphant, are they safe; the gun
Glanced just, and sudden, from the fowler's eye
O'ertakes their sounding pinions; and again,
Immediate, brings them from the towering wing,
Dead to the ground; or drives them wide-dispersed,
Wounded, and wheeling various, down the wind.

J. Thomson.

HUNTING.

Poor is the triumph o'er the timid hare!
Scared from the corn and now to some lone seat
Retired: the rushy fen; the ragged furze;
Stretch'd o'er the stony heath; the stubble chapp'd:
The thistly lawn; the thick-entangled broom;
Of the same friendly hue, the wither'd fern;
The fallow ground laid open to the sun,
Concoctive; and the nodding sandy bank,
Hung o'er the mazes of the mountain brook.
Vain is her best precaution, though she sits
Conceal'd with folded ears, unsleeping eyes,
By Nature raised to take the horizon in:

And head couch'd close betwixt her hairy feet,
In act to spring away. The scented dew
Betrays her early labyrinth; and deep,
In scatter'd sullen openings, far behind,
With every breeze she hears the coming storm.

But nearer and more frequent, as it loads
The sighing gale, she springs amazed, and all
The savage soul of game is up at once:
The pack full-opening, various, the shrill horn
Resounded from the hills; the neighing steed,
Wild for the chase: and the loud hunter's shout;
O'er a weak, harmless, flying creature, all
Mix'd in mad tumult, and discordant joy.

J. Thomson.

THE RISING OF THE SUN.

Wake! wake! wake to the hunting!
Wake ye, wake! the morning is nigh!
  Chilly the breezes blow
  Up from the sea below,
Chilly the twilight creeps over the sky!
Mark how fast the stars are fading!
Mark how wide the dawn is spreading!
  Many a fallow deer
  Feeds in the forest near;
Now is no time on the heather to lie!

Rise, rise! look on the ocean!
Rise ye, rise, and look on the sky!
  Softly the vapours sweep
  Over the level deep,
Softly the mists on the waterfall lie!
In the cloud red tints are glowing,
On the hill the black cock's crowing;
  And through the welkin red,
  See where he lifts his head,
(Forth to the hunting!) The sun's riding high!

Reginald Heber.

FADING FLOWERS.

HE purple iris hangs his head
  On his lean stalk, and so declines ;
The spider spills his silver thread
  Between the bells of columbines :
An alter'd light in flickering eves
  Draws dews thro' these dim eyes of ours ;
  Death walks in yonder waning bowers,
And burns the blistering leaves.
      Ah, well-a-day !
      Blooms overblow :
      Suns sink away :
      Sweet things decay.

The drunken beetle, roused ere night,
  Breaks blundering from the rotting rose,
Flits thro' blue spidery aconite,
  And hums, and comes, and goes :
His thick, bewilder'd song receives
  A drowsy sense of grief like ours :
  He hums and hums among the bowers,
And bangs about the leaves.
      Ah, well-a-day !
      Hearts overflow :
      Joy flits away :
      Sweet things decay.

Her yellow stars the jasmine drops
  In mildew'd mosses one by one :
The hollyhocks fall off their tops :
  The lotus-blooms all white i' the sun :
The freckled foxglove faints and grieves ;
  The smooth-paced slumbrous slug devours
  The glewy globes of gorgeous flowers,
And smears the glistering leaves.
      Ah, well-a-day !
      Life leaves us so :
      Love dare not stay :
      Sweet things decay.

From brazen sunflowers, orb and fringe,
  The burning burnish dulls and dies:
Sad Autumn sets a sullen tinge
  Upon the scornful peonies:
The dewy frog limps out, and heaves
  A speckled lump in speckled bowers:
  A reeking moisture clings, and lowers
The lips of lapping leaves.
        Ah, well-a-day!
        Ere the cock crow,
        Life's charm'd array
        Reels all away.

                             Owen Meredith.

THE LAST LEAF.

In spring and summer winds may blow,
  And rains fall after, hard and fast;
The tender leaves, if beaten low,
  Shine but the more for shower and blast.

But when their fated hour arrives,
  When reapers long have left the field,
When maidens rifle turn'd-up hives,
  And their last juice fresh apples yield,

A leaf perhaps may still remain
  Upon some solitary tree,
Spite of the wind and of the rain:
  A thing you heed not if you see.

At last it falls. Who cares? Not one:
  And yet no power on earth can ever
Replace the fallen leaf upon
  Its spray, so easy to dissever.

If such be love I dare not say,
  Friendship is such, too well I know,
I have enjoy'd my summer day;
  'Tis past; my leaf now lies below.   *W. S. Landor.*

P

WITHERED LEAVES.

DELICATE leaves, with your shifting colours,
    Crimson and golden, or russet brown,
Under what sunsets of calm October,
    Out of what groves were ye shaken down?

When the sun, dying in red and amber,
    Tinted the woods with the hues he wore,
As the stain'd light in a great cathedral,
    Through the east window, falls on the floor.

In your high homes where the tall shafts quiver,
    And the green boughs, like a trellis, cross,
When ye grow brighter, and change, and wither,
    Symbols ye are of our gain and loss.

Hopes that we cherish'd, and grand ideals,
    Dreams that to colour and substance grew,
Ah! they were lofty and green and golden,
    Now they lie dead on our hearts like you.

Silent as snow from his airy chamber,
    Down on the earth drops the wither'd leaf,
Silently back, on the heart of the dreamer,
    Noticed of none, falls the secret grief.

Yet ye deceive us, beautiful prophets;
    For like one side of an ocean shell,
Cast by the tide on a dripping sand-beach,
    Only a half of the truth ye tell.

Much of decadence and death ye sing us,
    Rightly ye tell us earth's hopes are vain,
But of the life out of death no whisper,
    Saying, 'We die, but we live again.'

Bring us some teacher, O leaves autumnal—
    Some voice to sing, from your crimson skies,
Of the home where our hope is immortal,
    Of the land where the leaf never dies.

                          C. F. Alexander.

THE DOG'S GRAVE.

LIE here, without a record of thy worth,
Beneath a covering of the common earth!
It is not from unwillingness to praise,
Or want of love, that here no stone we raise:
More thou deserv'st; but *this* man gives to man,
Brother to brother, *this* is all we can.
Yet they to whom thy virtues made thee dear
Shall find thee through all changes of the year:
This oak points out thy grave; the silent tree
Will gladly stand a monument of thee.

   We grieved for thee, and wished thy end were past
And willingly have laid thee here at last:
For thou hadst lived till everything that cheers
In thee had yielded to the weight of years;
Extreme old age had wasted thee away,
And left thee but a glimmering of the day;
Thy ears were deaf, and feeble were thy knees,—
I saw thee stagger in the summer breeze,

Too weak to stand against its sportive breath,
And ready for the gentlest stroke of death.
It came, and we were glad; yet tears were shed;
Both man and woman wept when thou wert dead;
Not only for a thousand thoughts that were
Old household thoughts, in which thou hadst thy share;
But for some precious boons vouchsafed to thee,
Found scarcely anywhere in like degree!
For love, that comes wherever life and sense
Are given by God, in thee was most intense;
A chain of heart, a feeling of the mind,
A tender sympathy, which did thee bind
Not only to us Men, but to thy Kind:
Yea, for thy fellow-brutes in thee we saw
A soul of love, love's intellectual law :—
Hence, if we wept, it was not done in shame;
Our tears from passion and from reason came,
And, therefore, shalt thou be an honoured name!

W. Wordsworth.

THE DEPARTURE OF THE BIRDS.

WHEN Autumn scatters his departing gleams,
    Warn'd of approaching Winter, gather'd play
    The swallow-people; and toss'd wide around,
    O'er the calm sky, in convolution swift,
    The feather'd eddy floats: rejoicing once,
        Ere to their wintry slumbers they retire;
In clusters clung, beneath the mouldering bank,
And where, unpierced by frost, the cavern sweats.
Or rather into warmer climes conveyed,
With other kindred birds of season, there
They twitter cheerful, till the vernal months
Invite them welcome back: for, thronging, now
Innumerous wings are in commotion all.

J. Thomson.

THE CHURCHYARD.

Our ancient church! its lonely tower,
   Beneath the loftier spire,
Is shadowed when the sunset hour
   Clothes the tall shaft in fire;
It sinks beyond the distant eye,
   Long ere the glittering vane,
High wheeling in the western sky,
   Has faded o'er the plain.

Like sentinel and nun, they keep
   Their vigil on the green;
One seems to guard, and one to weep,
   The dead that lie between;
And both roll out, so full and near,
   Their music's mingling waves,
They shake the grass, whose pennoned spear
   Leans on the narrow graves.

The stranger parts the flaunting weeds,
   Whose seeds the winds have strown
So thick beneath the line he reads,
   They shade the sculptured stone;
The child unveils his clustered brow,
   And ponders for a while
The graven willow's pendent bough,
   Or rudest cherub's smile.

But what to them the dirge, the knell?
   These were the mourner's share;—
The sullen clang, whose heavy swell
   Throbbed through the beating air;—
The rattling cord,—the rolling stone,—
   The shelving sand that slid,
And, far beneath, with hollow tone,
   Rung on the coffin's lid.

The slumberer's mound grows fresh and green,
  Then slowly disappears;
The mosses creep, the gray stones lean,
  Earth hides his date and years;
But, long before the once-loved name
  Is sunk or worn away,
No lip the silent dust may claim,
  That pressed the breathing clay.

Go where the ancient pathway guides,
  See where our sires laid down
Their smiling babes, their cherished brides,
  The patriarchs of the town;
Hast thou a tear for buried love?
  A sigh for transient power?
All that a century left above,
  Go, read it in an hour!

              O. Wendell Holmes.

THE CHURCHYARD.

WE walked within the churchyard bounds,
  My little boy and I—
He laughing, running happy rounds,
  I pacing mournfully.

"Nay, child! it is not well," I said,
  "Among the graves to shout,
To laugh and play amongst the dead,
  And make this noisy rout."

A moment to my side he clung;
  Leaving his merry play,
A moment stilled his joyous tongue,
  Almost as hushed as they;

Then, quite forgetting the command
  In life's exulting burst
Of early glee, let go my hand,
  Joyous as at the first.

And now I did not check him more,
  For, taught by Nature's face,
I had grown wiser than before,
  Even in that moment's space:

She spread no funeral pall above
  That patch of churchyard ground,
But the same azure vault of love
  As hung o'er all around.

And white clouds o'er that spot would pass,
  As freely as elsewhere;
The sunshine on no other grass
  A richer hue might wear.

And formed from out that very mould
  In which the dead did lie,
The daisy with its eye of gold
  Looked up into the sky.

The rook was wheeling overhead,
  Nor hastened to be gone—
The small bird did its glad notes shed,
  Perched on a gray head-stone.

And God, I said, would never give
  This light upon the earth,
Nor bid in childhood's heart to live
  These springs of gushing mirth,

If our one wisdom were to mourn,
  And linger with the dead,
To nurse, as wisest, thoughts forlorn
  Of worm and earthy bed.

O no! the glory earth puts on,
  The child's unchecked delight,
Both witness to a triumph won—
  (If we but read aright).

A triumph won o'er sin and death,
   From these the Saviour saves;
And, like a happy infant, Faith
   Can play among the graves.

Archbishop Trench.

THE CHURCH DIAL.

BENEATH me was the misty sea,
   O'er which a beetling summit hung,
And, half way up, a blasted tree
   With creaking branches swung:
The yellow crowsfoot blossomed there,
And juicy samphire to the bare
   And lean rock clung.

And sweetly to the very edge
   The soft and thymy greensward crept,
And, hanging slightly o'er the ledge,
   Perpetually wept
With drippings from a hidden spring,
Heard only when the murmuring
   Of ocean slept.

There, almost stooping o'er the wave,
   A rustic chapel stood; below
The sea had hollowed out a cave
   With labour long and slow;
And it was plain that any shock
That church from off its brow of rock
   Might overthrow.

And many a simple heart would grieve
   At this rude sacrilege of time,
Who loved for prayer, at noon or eve.
   The chalky downs to climb,
While to their litanies the wave,
With its eternal thunder, gave
   Response sublime.

So plaintively the soft sea wailed,
  So blue and breezy were the skies,
So tranquilly the white ships sailed
  In pomp before my eyes,
The very sweetness of it all
Did there my willing spirit call
  To moralize.

The dial on the chapel side
  With ivy tendrils was entwined,
As though the flight of time to hide
  Were office true and kind;
While, on the breath of ocean borne,
The restless shoots in playful scorn
  Waved unconfined.

This incident, the quiet hour,
  The sanctity of that lone place,
Conspired to give the sight a power
  Of true pathetic grace;
And, as I gazed on it, methought
That somewhat of a sign was wrought
  For me to trace.

For I interpreted the gesture,
  To illustrate how holy faith
Was the poor soul's unfading vesture,
  The saint's immortal wreath;
And, with significance sublime,
It taught how faith abolished time
  By killing death.

Mute preacher! pensive evergreen!
  O may I learn, this day, from thee,
The obscure sage of this lone scene
  Hard by the mighty sea,
How faith may, through Another's merit,
For all the sons of time inherit
  Eternity!

F. W. Faber.

Q

THE CLOSE OF AUTUMN.

THE melancholy days are come, the saddest of the year,
Of wailing winds and naked woods, and meadows brown and sere.
Heaped in the hollows of the grove the withered leaves lie dead,
They rustle to the eddying gust and to the rabbit's tread.
The robin and the wren are flown, and from the shrubs the jay,
And from the wood top calls the crow, through all the gloomy day.

Where are the flowers, the fair young flowers, that lately sprung and stood,
In brighter light and softer airs, a beauteous sisterhood?
Alas! they all are in their graves—the gentle race of flowers
Are lying in their lowly beds, with the fair and good of ours:
The rain is falling where they lie—but the cold November rain
Calls not from out the gloomy earth the lovely ones again.

The windflower and the violet, they perished long ago,
And the briar-rose and the orchis died, amid the summer's glow;
But on the hill the golden rod, and the aster in the wood,
And the yellow sunflower by the brook in autumn beauty stood,
Till fell the frost from the clear cold heaven, as falls the plague on men,
And the brightness of their smile was gone from upland, glade, and glen.

And now when comes the calm mild day—as still such days will come,
To call the squirrel and the bee from out their winter home;
When the sound of dropping nuts is heard, though all the trees are still,
And twinkle in the smoky light the waters of the rill,
The south wind searches for the flowers whose fragrance late he bore,
And sighs to find them in the wood and by the stream no more.

And then I think of one who in her youthful beauty died,
The fair meek blossom that grew up and faded by my side.
In the cold moist earth we laid her, when the forest cast the leaf,
And we wept that one so lovely should have had a lot so brief;
Yet not unmeet it was that one, like that young friend of ours,
So gentle and so beautiful, should perish with the flowers.

W. C. Bryant.

THE CLIFF.

AS slow I climb the cliff's ascending side,
  Much musing on the track of terror past,
  When o'er the dark wave rode the howling blast,
Pleased I look back, and view the tranquil tide
That laves the pebbled shores; and now the beam
  Of evening smiles on the gray battlement
  And yon forsaken tower that time has rent:
The lifted oar far off with silver gleam
Is touched, and the hushed billows seem to sleep.
  Soothed by the scene e'en thus on sorrow's breast
  A kindred stillness steals, and bids her rest;
Whilst sad airs stilly sigh along the deep,
Like melodies that mourn upon the lyre,
Waked by the breeze, and as they mourn expire.

W. L. Bowles.

THE SEA-GULLS.

By the grey sand-hills, o'er the cold sea-shore; where, dumbly peering,
Pass the pale-sail'd ships, scornfully, silently; wheeling, and veering
Swift out of sight again; while the wind searches what it finds never,
O'er the sand-reaches, bays, billows, blown beaches,—homeless for ever!
And, in a vision of the bare heaven seen and soon lost again,
Over the rolling foam, out in the mid-seas, round by the coast again,

Hovers the sea-gull, poised in the wind above, o'er the bleak surges,
In the green briny gleam, briefly reveal'd and gone; . . . fleet, as
    emerges
Out of the tumult of some brain where memory labours, and fretfully
Moans all the night long—a wild-winged hope, soon fading regretfully.

                     Owen Meredith.

THE FIELD MOUSE.

Wee, sleekit, cowrin', tim'rous beastie,
Oh, what a panic's in thy breastie!
Thou needna start awa' sae hasty,
        Wi' bickering brattle ! *
I wad be laith to rin and chase thee
        Wi' murd'ring pattle ! †

I'm truly sorry man's dominion
Has broken Nature's social union,
And justifies that ill opinion
        Which makes thee startle
At me, thy poor earth-born companion,
        And fellow-mortal !

I doubt na, whyles, ‡ but thou may thieve ;
What then ? poor beastie, thou maun live !
A daimen icker in a thrave §
        'S a sma' request :
I'll get a blessing wi' the lave, ‖
        And never miss't !

Thy wee bit housie, too, in ruin !
It's silly wa's the win's are strewin' !
And naething now to big ¶ a new ane
        O' foggage green !
And bleak December's winds ensuin',
        Baith snell ** and keen !

Thou saw the fields laid bare and waste,
And weary winter comin' fast,
And cozie here beneath the blast,
        Thou thought to dwell,
Till, crash ! the cruel coulter past
        Out through thy cell.

---

* Hurrying run.   † Pattle or pettle, the plough-spade.   ‡ Sometimes.
§ An ear of corn in a thrave—that is, twenty-four sheaves.   ‖ Remainder.
        ¶ Build.   ** Sharp.

That wee bit heap o' leaves and stibble
Has cost thee mony a weary nibble!
Now thou's turn'd out for a' thy trouble,
　　　　　　　But * house or hauld †
To thole ‡ the winter's sleety dribble,
　　　　　　And cranreuch § cauld;

But, Mousie, thou art no thy lane ‖
In proving foresight may be vain:
The best-laid schemes o' mice and men
　　　　　　Gang aft a-gley, ¶
And lea'e us nought but grief and pain
　　　　　　For promised joy.

Still thou art blest, compared wi' me!
The present only toucheth thee:
But, och! I backward cast my e'e
　　　　　　On prospects drear!
And forward, though I canna see,
　　　　　　I guess and fear.

　　　　　　　　　　　　R. Burns.

SNOW.

Snow, snow, beautiful snow,
Falling so widely on all below:
　As heavenly gifts do ever—
Filling each hollow among the hills,
Hiding the track of the frozen rills,
　Lost in the gushing river.

---

* Without.　　† Holding.　　‡ Endure.　　§ Hoar-frost.
　　　　　‖ Not alone.　　¶ Wrong.

Snow, snow, beautiful snow,
Lying so lightly on all below,
  Garden and field spread over,
White as a spotless winding-sheet;
The flowers are lifeless, and thus 'tis meet
  The face of the dead to cover.

Snow, snow, beautiful snow,
Melting so softly from all below,
  Into the cold earth sinking:
Soon thy last traces shall disappear,
And spring, with carpet of flowers, be here,
  And none of the snow be thinking.

Yet greener the hollows among the hills,
And fuller the flow of the sparkling rills,
  Since the snow with moisture fed them.
Thus when our lives shall melt away,
Fresh and bright would their influence stay,
  If in holy deeds we shed them.

Isa Craig.

THE MOON-RAINBOW.

For lo, what think you? suddenly
The rain and the wind ceased, and the sky
Received at once the full fruition
Of the moon's consummate apparition.
The black cloud-barricade was riven,
Ruined beneath her feet, and driven
Deep in the west; while, bare and breathless,
North and south and east lay ready
For a glorious thing, that, dauntless, deathless,
Sprang across them, and stood steady.
'Twas a moon-rainbow, vast and perfect,
From heaven to heaven extending, perfect
As the mother-moon's self, full in face.
It rose, distinctly at the base
With its seven proper colours chorded,
Which still, in the rising, were compressed,
Until at last, they coalesced.
And supreme the spectral creature lorded
In a triumph of whitest white,—
Above which intervened the night.
But above night too, like only the next,
The second of a wondrous sequence,
Reaching in rare and rarer frequence,
Till the heaven of heavens were circumflext,
Another rainbow rose, a mightier,
Fainter, flushier, and flightier.—
Rapture dying along its verge!
Oh, whose foot shall I see emerge,
Whose, from the straining topmost dark,
On to the keystone of that arc?

R. Browning.

THE RAVEN.

UNDERNEATH an old oak tree
　　There was of swine a huge company,
That grunted as they crunched the mast;
For that was ripe, and fell full fast.
Then they trotted away, for the wind grew high:
One acorn they left, and no more might you spy.
Next came a raven, that liked not such folly:
He belonged, they did say, to the witch Melancholy!
Blacker was he than blackest jet,
Flew low in the rain, and his feathers not wet.
He picked up the acorn and buried it straight ·
By the side of a river both deep and great.
　　Where then did the raven go?
　　He went high and low,
Over hill, over dale, did the black raven go.
　　Many autumns, many springs
　　Travelled he with wandering wings:
　　Many summers, many winters—
　　I can't tell half his adventures.
At length he came back, and with him a she,
And the acorn was grown to a tall oak tree,
They built them a nest in the topmost bough,
And young ones they had, and were happy enow.
But soon came a woodman in leathern guise,
His brow, like a pent-house, hung over his eyes.
He'd an axe in his hand, not a word he spoke,
But with many a hem! and a sturdy stroke,
At length he brought down the poor raven's own oak.
His young ones were killed; for they could not depart,
And their mother did die of a broken heart.
The boughs from the trunk the woodman did sever;
And they floated it down on the course of the river.
They sawed it in planks, and its bark they did strip,
And with this tree and others they made a good ship.

R

The ship, it was launched; but in sight of the land
Such a storm there did rise as no ship could withstand.
It bulged on a rock, and the waves rushed in fast:
Round and round flew the raven, and cawed to the blast.
He heard the last shriek of the perishing souls—
See! See! o'er the topmast the mad water rolls!

   Right glad was the raven, and off he went fleet,
And Death riding home on a cloud he did meet,
And he thank'd him again and again for this treat:
   They had taken his all, and revenge it was sweet.

                           S. T. Coleridge.

THE FOUR DOGS.

On his morning rounds the Master
Goes to learn how all things fare;
Searches pasture after pasture,
Sheep and cattle eyes with care;
And, for silence or for talk,
He hath comrades in his walk;
Four dogs, each pair of different breed,
Distinguished two for scent, and two for speed.

See a hare before him started!
———Off they fly in earnest chase;
Every dog is eager-hearted,
All the four are in the race:
And the hare whom they pursue,
Knows from instinct what to do;
Her hope is near; no turn she makes;
But, like an arrow, to the river takes.

Deep the river was, and crusted
Thinly by a one-night's frost;
But the nimble Hare hath trusted
To the ice, and safely cross'd;

She hath cross'd, and without heed
All are following at full speed,
When, lo! the ice, so thinly spread,
Breaks—and the greyhound, Dart, is overhead!

Better fate have Prince and Swallow—
See them cleaving to the sport!
Music has no heart to follow,
Little Music, she stops short.
She hath neither wish nor heart,
Hers is now another part:
A loving creature she, and brave!
And fondly strives her struggling friend to save.

From the brink her paws she stretches,
Very hands as you would say!
And afflicting moans she fetches,
As he breaks the ice away.
For herself she hath no fears,—
Him alone she sees and hears,—
Makes efforts with complainings; nor gives o'er
Until her fellow sinks to reappear no more.

W. Wordsworth.

WATER-FOWL.

MARK how the feathered tenants of the flood,
With grace of motion that might scarcely seem
Inferior to angelical, prolong
Their curious pastime! shaping in mid air
(And sometimes with ambitious wing that soars
High as the level of the mountain tops)
A circuit ampler than the lake beneath—
Their own domain; but ever, while intent
On tracing and retracing that large round,
Their jubilant activity evolves

Hundreds of curves and circlets, to and fro,
Upward and downward, progress intricate
Yet unperplexed, as if one spirit swayed
Their indefatigable flight. 'Tis done—
Ten times, or more, I fancied it had ceased;
But lo! the vanished company again
Ascending; they approach—I hear their wings,

Faint, faint at first; and then an eager sound,
Pass'd in a moment—and as faint again!
They tempt the sun to sport amid their plumes;
They tempt the water, or the gleaming ice,
To show them a fair image; 'tis themselves,
Their own fair forms, upon the glimmering plain,
Painted more soft and fair as they descend
Almost to touch;—then up again aloft,
Up with a sally and a flash of speed,
As if they scorned both resting-place and rest!

                 W. Wordsworth.

THE WILD FOWL'S VOICE.

It chanced upon the merry merry Christmas eve,
  I went sighing past the church across the moorlands dreary—
O! never sin and want and woe this earth will leave,
  And the bells but mock the wailing sound, they sing so cheery.

How long, O Lord! how long, before Thou come again?
  Still in cellar, and in garret, and on mountain dreary,
The orphans moan, and widows weep, and poor men toil in vain,
  Till earth is sick of hope deferr'd, though Christmas bells be cheery.

Then arose a joyous clamour, from the wild fowl on the mere,
  Beneath the stars, across the snow, like clear bells ringing,
And a voice within cried—"Listen! Christmas carols even here,
  Though thou be dumb, yet o'er their work, the stars and snows are
    singing.

Blind!—I live, I love, I reign; and all the nations through,
  With the thunder of My judgments even now are ringing;
Do thou fulfil thy work, but as yon wild fowl do,
  Thou wilt heed no less the wailing, yet hear through it angels
    singing."

C. Kingsley.

THE BIRDS IN WINTER.

Now from the roost, or from the neighbouring pale,
Where, diligent to catch the first faint gleam
Of smiling day, they gossiped side by side,
Come trooping at the housewife's well-known call
The feather'd tribes domestic. Half on wing,
And half on foot, they brush the fleecy flood,

Conscious and fearful of too deep a plunge.
The sparrows peep, and quit the sheltering eaves
To seize the fair occasion. Well they eye
The scattered grain, and thievishly resolved
To escape the impending famine, often scared
As oft return, a pert voracious kind.
Clean riddance quickly made, one only care
Remains to each, the search of sunny nook,
Or shed impervious to the blast. Resigned
To sad necessity the cock foregoes
His wonted strut; and wading at their head
With well-considered steps, seems to resent
His altered gait and stateliness entrenched.
How find the myriads, that in summer cheer
The hills and valleys with their ceaseless songs,
Due sustenance, or where subsist they now?
Earth yields them nought; the imprisoned worm is safe
Beneath the frozen clod; all seeds of herbs
Lie covered close; and berry-bearing thorns
That feed the thrush (whatever some suppose)
Afford the smaller minstrels no supply.

W. Cowper.

FROST.

AT eve,
Steam'd eager from the red horizon round,
With the fierce rage of winter deep suffused,
An icy gale, oft shifting, o'er the pool
Breathes a blue film, and in its mid career
Arrests the bickering stream. The loosened ice,
Let down the flood, and half dissolved by day,
Rustles no more; but to the sedgy bank
Fast grows, or gathers round the pointed stone,
A crystal pavement, by the breath of heaven
Cemented firm, till, seized from shore to shore,
The whole imprison'd river growls below.
Loud rings the frozen earth, and hard reflects
A double noise; while at his evening watch,

The village dog deters the nightly thief;
The heifer lows; the distant waterfall
Swells in the breeze; and, with the hasty tread
Of traveller, the hollow-sounding plain
Shakes from afar. The full ethereal round,
Infinite worlds disclosing to the view,
Shines out intensely keen; and, all one cope
Of starry glitter, glows from pole to pole.
From pole to pole the rigid influence falls,
Thro' the still night, incessant, heavy, strong,
And seizes nature fast. It freezes on;
Till morn, late-rising o'er the drooping world,
Lifts her pale eye unjoyous. Then appears
The various labour of the silent night:
Prone from the dripping eave, and dumb cascade,
Whose idle torrents only seem to roar,
The pendent icicle; the frost-work fair,
Where transient hues, and fancied figures rise;
Wide-spouted o'er the hill, the frozen brook,
A livid tract, cold-gleaming on the morn;
The forest bent beneath the plumy wave;

And by the frost refined the whiter snow,
Incrusted hard, and sounding to the tread
Of early shepherd, as he pensive seeks
His pining flock, or from the mountain top,
Pleased with the slippery surface, swift descends,

J. Thomson.

WOODS IN WINTER.

WHEN winter winds are piercing chill,
　　And through the hawthorn blows the gale,
With solemn feet I tread the hill,
　　That overbrows the lonely vale.

O'er the bare upland, and away
　　Through the long reach of desert woods,
The embracing sunbeams chastely play,
　　And gladden these deep solitudes.

Where, twisted round the barren oak,
　　The summer vine in beauty clung,
And summer winds the stillness broke,
　　The crystal icicle is hung.

Where, from their frozen urns, mute springs
　　Pour out the river's gradual tide,
Shrilly the skater's iron rings,
　　And voices fill the woodland side.

Alas! how changed from the fair scene,
　　When birds sang out their mellow lay,
And winds were soft, and woods were green,
　　And the song ceased not with the day.

But still wild music is abroad,
    Pale, desert woods! within your crowd;
And gathering winds, in hoarse accord,
    Amid the vocal reeds pipe loud.

Chill airs and wintry winds! my ear
    Has grown familiar with your song;
I hear it in the opening year,—
    I listen, and it cheers me long.

H. W. Longfellow.

THE SEASONS.

So forth issued the Seasons of the year;
First, lusty Spring, all dight in leaves and flowers
That freshly budded, and new blossoms did bear,
In which a thousand birds had built their bowers,
That sweetly sung to call forth paramours;
And in his hand a javelin he did bear,
And on his head (as fit for warlike stours)
A gilt engraven morion he did wear,
That as some did him love, so others did him fear.

Then came the jolly Summer, being dight
In a thin silken cassock coloured green
That was unlined all, to be more light,
And on his head a garland well beseen
He wore, from which, as he had chafed been,
The sweat did drop, and in his hand he bore
A bow and shaft, as he in forest green
Had hunted late the libbard or the boar,
And now would bathe his limbs, with labour heated sore.

s

Then came the Autumn, all in yellow clad,
　　As though he joyed in his plenteous store,
Laden with fruits that made him laugh, full glad
　　That he had banished Hunger, which tofore
　　Had by the belly oft him pinched sore;
Upon his head a wreath, that was enroled
　　With ears of corn of every sort, he bore,
And in his hand a sickle he did hold,
To reap the ripened fruits the which the earth had yold.

Lastly came Winter, clothed all in frieze,
　　Chattering his teeth for cold that did him chill,
Whilst on his hoary beard his breath did freeze,
　　And the dull drops that from his purpled bill
　　As from a limbeck did adown distil;
In his right hand a tipped staff he held,
　　With which his feeble steps he stayed still,
For he was faint with cold and weak with eld
That scarce his loosed limbs he able was to weld.

E. Spenser.

INDEX.